The Arrangement

Book one in the Seattle Billionaires series

Nora Ford

Chapter One
Talia

I just got off the phone with my mother. It was the third time today, and it was driving me crazy. Though I kept telling her that it's a business meeting and not a date, she doesn't get it. She was so excited about my meeting this evening and checked in with me every couple of hours.

However, every time she used a different excuse for her call, this time she told me that Timo, my son, ate his supper and was playing in the garden. That was clever of her because my son is top of my priority list and my work comes second, what she refuses to understand is that men are not on this list at all.

Since my divorce six years ago I've sworn off men for good. My mom won't accept that though.

I have a great family; they are loving, caring and supportive. Although I didn't follow in my father's footsteps and didn't study medicine like my sisters, they weren't disappointed.

When I dropped out of college and left everything behind to move with my husband to England, they respected my choice although they weren't happy about it.

When I came back a year later, broke, pregnant and with no college degree, they never said 'we told you so'. They encouraged me to start over and even financed my courses in graphics and web design, after my ex-husband took every cent of my trust fund.

They taught all three of us that one has to love what one does to excel. That is what I do, I love my work, and I am good at it. With my son and my work, I don't have time or energy for anything else, and I like my life the way it is. However, my parents and sisters worry about me all the time.

As much as I love them all, they can be a pain in the ass sometimes. My mom wants all her daughters to have what she has with my father, a perfect marriage. They have been married for thirty years now, and they still love each other dearly. But it's a gift not everyone can have.

They fell in love and got married in England, while my dad was in his first year of residency.

My mom was a nurse at the same hospital. Shortly after my elder sister, Olivia was born, she quit her job to become a full-time wife and mother. Although she loved her career, she was happy with her role as a wife and a mother.

When my dad decided to return to the States a few years later, my mom left her country, her family, and her friends and came here with him. That was twenty years ago, she never regretted it. She always says with the right person one can be happy anywhere.

She is probably right, but the right person doesn't always exist. I learned that the hard way. When I caught myself thinking about my painful marriage experience, I quickly pushed the memories from my mind. I stood up and began preparing for my meeting.

Two hours later, I was dressed to the nines and sitting in my car on my way to the restaurant, where this meeting was going to take place. I don't meet with clients outside their offices, but Adam Grant was an exception.

He is a legend when it comes to money and success. He was only twenty-four when he took over his father's investment company. In a little less than ten years, he turned it into an Empire.

He is now one of the wealthiest men in the States; he was only thirty-two when he made it to the Forbes billionaires list. He radiates charisma. Everything about him is public news. Like everyone, I read that he recently broke up his engagement. Although I wasn't interested in his personal life, a story like that was everywhere.

I tried to make an appointment with him for weeks, but it was hopeless. So, I decided to take another approach. I stormed into his office last week dressed in jeans and a hoodie. I knew I had only a few minutes before security arrived, but all I wanted was to attract his attention, and I did. I left him my proposal and contact numbers and left before his assistant could return with the security guard.

I knew I was taking a risk, but I had nothing to lose. My proposal would end up in the trash bin if it went through the conventional channels. I couldn't believe it when Adam's assistant called to arrange the meeting. I didn't hesitate and instantly agreed.

I desperately need the money I will make doing work for him. Most of my clients are small business owners, who need my help to set their web pages or online shops. After I do the initial settings for them, they do the rest themselves. This wouldn't be a problem if I had new clients every day, but this isn't the case.

I need to do some work for bigger companies, which would regularly use my services, so I can maintain a reasonable income and can pay my bills.

My parents won't mind helping me with the bills, but I don't want that, I need to be able to do it on my own. I am twenty-seven, and I find it awkward asking them for money. If everything goes well this evening, I won't need their financial support.

Walking into the restaurant, a young waitress welcomed me. When I told her my name, she politely accompanied me to Adam's table. I've never been here before, but I've heard about it. People wait for weeks to get a table. However, I don't think Adam had to wait. Some rules don't apply to everyone.

Chapter Two
Talia

Adam was already seated and checking something on his phone. I instantly saw him, the way he filled out his designer suit took my breath away. *This is a business meeting,* I reminded myself.

He noticed me and stood as I approached. A wave of heat surged over me when he reached out and took my hand in his. His penetrating stare and confident smile quivered as we shook hands.

"Ms. Jones, thanks for meeting me on such short notice." His eyes scanned me from head to toe and a small smile touched the corners of his mouth. From the expression on Adam's face, I could tell that he liked what he saw.

I offered him a smile as I removed my hand from his. "I don't normally meet with clients outside their office, but..." before I could finish my sentence, he said with a grin. "For me, you made an exception, everyone does, but I appreciate it anyway."

I didn't know how to respond to this arrogant comment. So, I chose to let it slide. To hide my nervousness, I buried my face in the menu in front of me thinking, *Things aren't going as planned.* Adam dominated the space by simply being there.

Much to my relief, the waitress came and took our orders. After she left, I asked him, "So, what do you think of my proposal?"

"Sorry, but I haven't had a chance to look at it yet."

"If you haven't read my proposal, what's the point of this meeting?" I asked confused.

"I have another offer for you, and I think it would be much more lucrative." He smiled widely, exposing his perfect teeth.

This conversation was going all wrong, and I didn't like it, but trying to sound casual, asked, "What kind of offer?"

Before he could answer, the waitress came with our orders. Although I wasn't hungry, I tried to distract myself with the food in front of me. I was hoping he wouldn't notice how nervous he was making me.

After the waitress left, we ate in silence for a few moments, then he finally said, "It's an unusual offer, one you won't get every day. I want your exclusive services for a year, and I am going to pay you $100,000 a month. On top of that you'll get a million dollars in cash when the year ends to my satisfaction."

I could feel his eyes on me all the time. He was carefully studying my reaction to his words. I didn't know how he was expecting me to respond and I honestly didn't care. One thing was clear though: this meeting was a huge mistake I was about to correct.

I opened my purse and took out my credit card, but he stopped me before I could call the waitress.

"What are you doing?" he wanted to know.

"I am paying for my food. Thanks for your offer but I am not a call girl Mr. Grant." I answered, while I was searching for the waitress who took our orders.

"Now you're insulting me," he said sounding upset.

"We're even then," I said shortly. I was still scanning for the waitress and couldn't find her anywhere.

"You've got me wrong; I didn't mean it that way. Believe it or not but I don't have to pay for sex. Besides, sex is the last thing I want from you," he said with a grin this time.

I don't know why I felt this way, but I was upset. Not that I wanted to have sex with him, but the fact that he didn't find me attractive bruised my ego. However, I didn't show it and just asked him, "Then what do you want from me, Mr. Grant?"

"Adam, please, and I want to marry you," he said simply.

"Sorry, what did you say?" I asked confused.

"You heard me right the first time. I want to marry you. If you say yes, we will get married this Friday." I could see my reaction amused him.

"Sorry, but I don't understand," I said confused.

"You must have heard about my engagement to the senator's daughter and the scandalous photos of her and her new boyfriend while wearing my ring."

He looked me in the eye to make sure he had my attention, and then went on, "She is doing this on purpose to embarrass me. I gave a statement and said that I broke off the engagement, but it's not enough. I need to get married soon. So, I'll give the press something else to talk about."

"I still don't get it; you broke up with her, why do her news and photos affect you?" I asked again.

He took a deep breath and tried to explain again. "Everything about me is news. Negative publicity doesn't only affect my image in the market, it also scares small investors and makes them sell their stocks and shares in my companies. I am losing money with every photo she publishes. So, I need to act quickly."

"I see now, but why me? Wouldn't a young model or someone prominent be a better choice?" I suggested.

He shook his head, "No, I thought about that, but it would scare the shareholders even more. They would think I am spending their hard-earned money on a gold-digger," he explained, but I wasn't convinced.

"You, on the other hand, are a perfect choice. You belong to the upper middle class, and you come from a respectable family. You will represent stability and people will love you."

I nodded, "Okay, I see your point but won't you have this problem again when we get divorced."

He shook his head and said. "No, we are going to come up with a good reason for the divorce, like the fact that I'm a workaholic and married to my company. This way I'll gain the trust of the shareholder, and you'll gain the sympathy of the people. It's going to be good for you as well."

He was waiting for me to respond, and when I didn't, he took out a business card from his pocket and gave it to me. "I have to leave now but here are the contact details of my publicist."

When I made a perplexed expression, he added, "He is the one responsible for my websites, logos, and all those things. If you decide to refuse my offer, you can still contact him with your proposal. I am sure he will be glad to work with you."

"Does this mean I can still do work for you even if I say no?" I asked cautiously.

"Yes, but if you decide to accept, I will be waiting for you in my office tomorrow at ten. However, at ten thirty this offer will be off the table. I hope you will make the right choice."

He signaled the waitress to bring the check, this time she came running. After he paid, he rose up and just left.

Chapter Three
Talia

I sat there speechless and confused by his offer. I didn't know how to react to this insane proposition. I probably should forget about it and call his publicist. A chance was all I wanted to gain from this meeting, and I got it. So why the hell do I think about this crazy deal?

I was still wrapped up in my thoughts when the waitress came to ask me if I wanted something else. I politely declined and grabbed my purse to leave. On my way out, I noticed that other guests were staring at me. "Great. One meeting with Adam Grant and people start talking," I murmured to myself walking to my car.

Before I left the parking lot, I called my mom and asked her if Timo could spend the night. I knew she would love to have him, but still, I had to ask. After I hung up the phone with my mother, I drove to my sister's apartment. I needed someone to talk to, and I couldn't think of anyone other than one of my sisters.

My sisters and I are best friends; we can tell each other any and everything. We're close to our mom too, however, I can't discuss this arrangement with my mom; her answer would be a big NO. She believes in love, and forever, a wife for rent isn't her kind of thing.

Olivia, my older sister, isn't an option, she is married, and I don't get along with her husband. So, Tessa, my younger sister is the better choice. She is only two years younger than me, and she is a good listener. She is a second-year resident doctor, specializing in Gynecology and Obstetrics, and she works crazy hours.

On my way I stopped to buy some essential groceries, I knew her fridge would probably be empty. I had a key to her apartment, but I was praying she would be home. I didn't bother to ring just used my key. If she was home, she would probably be sleeping.

She wasn't there, but I decided to wait for her. I was putting the groceries away in the fridge when I heard the door close.

"Tal!" I heard her calling.

"In here," I answered.

"Hi, what are you doing here?" she asked.

"I am stuffing your fridge, what else?" I said.

"Thanks, if it weren't for you, mom and Liv, I would starve." She gave me a weak smile. She looked exhausted.

"Why are you doing this to yourself?" I wanted to know.

"This is the price you have to pay to be a resident doctor," she shrugged.

"Yes, but you look like shit," I was stating a fact.

"Thanks for pointing it out, I feel like shit too. I wish I could say the same about you, but you look gorgeous tonight. A hot date?" She grinned.

"No, a business meeting," I said shortly. She gave me a suspicious look and asked, "You're dressed like this for a business meeting?"

"Go take a shower and change these scrubs, while I fix you something to eat and then we'll talk," I suggested.

She frowned and said, "You sound serious, but you're right I need to shower first so that I can feel like a human again. See you in a few."

"Take your time," I told her on her way out.

I quickly went to change into a pair of sweatpants and a t-shirt. I always leave a few things for Timo and myself here and at my parents. It's practical and efficient. Half an hour later, I had set the kitchen table, and was waiting for Tessa. She came in a few moments later dressed in a sleep shirt. "Coffee please," she said.

"No, eat something first. I can't believe you're a doctor and have all these unhealthy habits. You should set an example for your patients," I scolded.

"I tell my patients to do as I say not as I do. Besides, I am not pregnant; I can drink as much coffee as I want," she shrugged.

"You might not be pregnant now, but you'll be someday. You should take better care of yourself," I argued.

She shook her head, gave me a weak smile and said, "Not anytime soon."

"It's been two years; you must start living again." I gently patted her shoulder.

Tessa lost her fiancé in a car accident two years ago. Although she tries to hide it, she's still grieving.

"Now stop acting like a mom and tell me what's wrong?" she changes the subject.

I let it slide and said, "Okay, eat something first, and I'll tell you everything while you're eating."

She nodded and bit into her sandwich. "Now tell," she said with a mouth full of food.

I told her everything. I started with how I was trying to make an appointment with Adam Grant for weeks without any success, the stunt I pulled at his office last week, the meeting and finally his crazy offer.

Tessa was listening carefully; she didn't interrupt me even once. When I finished, she gave me a knowing look and said, "So, you want to accept his offer."

"I didn't say that," I said quickly.

"It's obvious, if you are not considering it, you won't be here," She shrugged.

"I couldn't just ignore an offer like that," I said almost to myself.

"So, you're considering it," She repeated.

"It's not the money, although it's a lot. The publicity, the connections, do you know what this means, it's the breakthrough that I need." I was thinking aloud now.

"You may be right, but at what cost Tal?" She asked.

"What cost? I'll marry the richest, hottest bachelor in Seattle for twelve months, what's wrong with that?" I said trying to sound convincing.

"People don't plan their divorce before they get married and you know it," she tried to talk sense into me.

"Now you sound like mom, besides I've tried the real thing before and it didn't last long either," I said trying to shake off the memories of my first marriage.

"You were too young back then; it wasn't your fault."

Jeff, my ex-husband was an assistant doctor my dad was training; he charmed his way into every heart in my family. I wasn't immune to his charm; I fell in love with him. He was ten years older than me, but I didn't mind the age difference. I liked the fact that he was experienced and mature.

Shortly after we married, dad arranged a post for him in one of London's hospitals, I left everything behind, and moved there with him. Before long I realized that all he was after was my dad's connections and money.

When I refused to ask my parents for money, he started to show me his ugly side. He didn't abuse me physically, but emotionally. Although he was discrete about his affairs, he made sure that I knew about every single one of them. After I fell pregnant, things got worse. He didn't want the baby; he said we couldn't afford a baby on only one income.

He demanded that I either end my pregnancy or ask my parents for financial support. I didn't like the options he gave me, so that day I booked a ticket back to the States, and we divorced a few months later.

"I was twenty not sixteen, I should have known better," I said, pushing the painful memories from my mind. Tessa didn't respond, she just gave me a sympathetic look. I shook my head and said, "I don't regret it, I have my son. I won't trade him for the world."

"Speaking of Timo, have you thought about how this deal is going to affect him?" she asked.

"He won't be affected; he won't even notice any difference. Adam is a very busy man; he won't be around most of the time. This is a fake marriage remember; feelings are not involved. So, Timo won't have to share me with another man. He will remain my one and only," I explained.

"There is nothing wrong with Timo sharing you if it is with the right guy," she gave me a warm smile.

"Right guys don't exist," I said shortly.

She ignored my last statement and asked, "Are you sure this is going to be safe?"

"What do you mean?" I didn't understand her question.

"I mean are you sure he's not in any kinky stuff?" She asked concerned.

"Do you mean the Fifty Shades of Grey kind of things?" I asked amused.

"Yes, and why are you grinning? These things exist," she said.

"I am not sure about that, but I am sure about one thing, he is not interested in me in that way. He made it clear that this marriage will be on paper only. So, no sex, kinky or not," I assured her.

"You made up your mind; you're going to accept." She was stating a fact, and she was right.

Chapter Four
Adam

The next day, I sat in my office waiting for Talia. I was hoping she would come. Something about her challenges me, she radiates original beauty. Nothing about her is fake.

Her stunning blue eyes and warm chestnut hair which flows over her shoulders were enough to knock a man's breath from his lungs. She is tall and has a slender body. The fact that she is unaware of her prettiness made her even more beautiful.

However, I was attracted to her spirit and courage rather than her physical beauty. *She will show up,* I assured myself.

Although Talia was different than my former fiancé, she is a woman and money drives women. I had a lot of affairs before with models, starlets and politician's daughters. Every one of them was unique in a certain way, but they all have two things in common: they always want more, and they can't be trusted.

I took a last look at the prenup contract that my legal team prepared earlier this week, and I was satisfied. It was a generous one, but it also ensured that she won't sue me for anything more in the future. I have trust issues, and I don't trust women.

Everything was ready for the meeting, the contract and the draft that I wrote about the topics we need to discuss today. One thing was missing though, Talia.

It was ten-twenty, and she wasn't here yet. I grabbed the list of the other candidates and looked at it quickly. They were all attractive women, one or two of them were even more beautiful than Talia, however, I don't want any of them; I want her. I wasn't bluffing when I said the offer wouldn't stand beyond ten-thirty, though. I am a very busy and very impatient man; I don't like to be kept waiting.

I was debating who I would call next, when I heard my assistant's voice through the intercom saying, "Ms. Jones is here to see you, Sir."

"Let her in and cancel my next meeting," I said shortly.

Before I could reach the door to welcome her myself, she entered my office. I didn't understand how she could look so sexy wearing a pair of skinny black jeans and an oversize crème pullover.

She didn't bother with greeting me, chastising, she said, "That was rude, hasn't your mother taught you to say 'please' and 'thank you'?"

For a moment I was confused, no one has ever accused me of being rude, yet they always wanted something from me. I just shook my head and answered, "My mom had other things in mind than teaching me manners." She didn't know about my relationship to my mother, and I wanted to keep it that way.

I extended my hand to shake hers, but she didn't take it. Instead, she leaned in and gave me a quick kiss on the cheek. Not only her friendly attitude surprised me but also the way I reacted to her simple kiss. It was electrifying. I managed to hide my surprise.

"Sorry, I am late. I was planning to be here on time, but the roads were too busy. Please don't think I'm trying to play hard to get," she simply said.

Again, she managed to surprise me; I didn't expect this kind of honesty. So, I spared her the lecture about how busy I am and just said, "It's okay, you're still on time." I gave her a copy of the prenup and the draft I wrote earlier. "We have a few points to discuss. I wrote everything here."

She took the papers I gave her and said, "I have a couple of points I'd like to discuss with you too, but I didn't write them down. We can go through your list first."

She took a seat on the couch in the seating area of my office. After she quickly scanned my list, she said, "Well as for number one; I don't need your shopper or stylist. Believe it or not, I know how to dress. I have a well-stocked wardrobe, but I am willing to add a few items to it. I'll buy them myself, however."

Before I could object, she turned to number two. "What's wrong with my car?"

"You can't be married to me and drive a fifteen years old car," I said impatiently.

"How do you know that? No, don't answer that. It's stupid to ask. You probably have a file on me," she asked and answered herself.

"You're right; I know everything about you," I confirmed.

"In that case, you must know about my car accident record. I guess you won't give me your Bugatti," she gave me an amused smile.

When I hesitated, she shook her head and said, "Don't worry, I don't want your Bugatti. I will buy a car, nothing fancy but new."

"Your new car will be delivered to your home this afternoon, consider it a wedding present," I said dismissing the subject.

"Thanks, but I can't accept it. First, this is a fake wedding, second, you're paying me well enough to afford a car. Besides, you don't want me to look like a spoiled rich man's wife. It's better for your image," she said and moved quickly to the third point.

"Number three is a deal breaker," I heard her saying. I looked at the list in my hands and frowned. Number three says that I'm going to hire a qualified nanny for her son.

"I don't understand, what is wrong with having a nanny? It's going to free your time and give you more flexibility," I asked confused.

"I'm a full-time mom, and I intend to stay that way. I won't accompany you on your business trips, dinners, and events unless my mom or one of my sisters will take care of Timo for me. If you have a problem with that, you have to find someone else." Her tone was relaxed but decisive.

I felt it was a take it or leave it deal, although I hate these kinds of deals, I nodded and said, "I can live with that." I looked at my list and told her, "The next topic would be your ex-husband."

"What about him?" She looked puzzled.

"Well, is he going to cause any problems in the future? It's not an issue but I need to know so that I can prepare myself," I told her.

"No, he won't cause any problems" she assured me.

"How can you be so sure?" I inquired.

She took a deep breath and told me,

"Fine, to cut the story short, he married me for the money, I was twenty-one when we got divorced, he took all the money that was in my trust fund, in return he gave up all his legal rights to see or contact his son."

She looked at me and explained, "Timor has my maiden name. We don't have any relationship with him anymore. He is out of the picture for good."

"And you gave him everything without a fight?" I couldn't believe it.

"I got the better part of the deal, I got my son," she said proudly.

I didn't know how to respond to that so I just nodded.

After a few moments, she smiled and said, "Good, the next point would be the wedding party this Friday. It's impossible for my mom to plan a wedding in four days," she sighed.

"That won't be a problem, I have a capable PR team, they will do all the work," I assured her.

"Fine, I will leave that to you and your PR team then. Since the wedding is going to take place at my parents' house, they have to contact my mom. But it has to wait until tomorrow," she told me.

When I nodded, she moved to our last point, the contract. She picked up a pen from the table in front of her and just signed the two copies and gave me mine.

"How could you sign something without reading it carefully first?" I was shocked.

"I trust you," she shrugged.

I shook my head still not believing what she had just done, "You shouldn't trust anybody."

"Good thing we're getting married, you can teach me how to mistrust people, and I will show you how to trust them," she suggested.

My trust issues were deeply rooted, but I didn't tell her that.

"We have covered my list; now it's your turn," I said changing the subject.

"I have two points. First, I still want to do work for you. If you like my work, your companies will keep using my services even after the divorce," she said.

"You've got it. I'll have my legal team put this in writing." I instantly agreed.

"Not necessary, your word is enough," she gave me a genuine smile.

I wanted to point out that she should be more careful but I didn't argue. Instead, I asked, "What is your second point?"

She hesitated, for a moment I thought she was going to ask for more money. Then she finally said, "Are you… are you going to have affairs? I mean twelve to eighteen months could be a long time and you…"

"And I might want to have sex. Is that what you're trying to say," I finished the sentence for her.

She didn't answer, she just nodded.

"I am not seeing anyone at the moment, but if I had an affair during our marriage, I would let you know first, and I will be very discrete about it," I assured her.

"Good, I can be very discrete too," she simply said.

I was horrified by her remark, I instantly asked, "Are you seeing someone?"

"No, but I want both of us to be on the same page. I am an equal partner in this relationship, and I expect to have the same rights," she warned me.

I wasn't prepared for that, but she had a point. I can't sleep around and expect her to be faithful.

"Fine, no affairs either of us," I finally said.

"Everything is settled then. I'll leave you to your work," she rose up to leave.

Before she reached the door, I stopped her by saying, "You can buy your car today if you want. I have transferred two months payment to your account."

She shook her head and said, "You shouldn't do that, I could run now with your money."

Without waiting for my answer, she opened the door and left.

Chapter Five
Talia

The days before the wedding were crazy; I had a hundred things to do. Telling my mom was on top of my to-do list, so I did it right after leaving Adam's office, and it wasn't fun. I didn't want to lie to her, but I didn't tell her the whole truth either. Although I didn't mention the money or the fact that the marriage is temporary, she wasn't pleased about rushing things.

Sure, she wanted me to get married, but this isn't what she was hoping for. She had this irrational, romantic idea about Adam and me. In her scenario; I would do work for him, we would get to know each other better, fall in love and then get married. I told her that wasn't the way things worked these days, and love is highly overrated.

However, I assured her that I wouldn't get hurt this time. "I am walking into this marriage with open eyes and mind."

She wasn't convinced, but she wished me luck and left me to tell my dad. She knew he would be disappointed; she was right.

Dad was in his study. He put what he was reading to the side when he heard me coming. I told him what I told my mom, that this marriage was a business deal: Adam would gain the family-man image he needed, in return, I work for his companies, and this is an excellent opportunity for me.

He couldn't hide his pain; my dad hasn't forgiven himself for my first marriage. Although he was against it because of the age difference, he still believes he was responsible since he was the one who introduced me to my ex-husband.

I gave him a big hug, then I looked into his eyes and said, "For the hundredth time, it wasn't your fault, Daddy. It was all me; it was all me."

Before he could object, I added, "Maybe I am not marrying for love this time, but I am marrying a better man." That wasn't a lie, Adam may be arrogant and overconfident, but I believed he was honest and fair.

My dad sighed and said, "I don't want to see you hurt again."

"I won't be, I promise," I reassured him, and I was determined to keep my promise. As long as no feelings were involved, I wouldn't get hurt. I kept repeating this sentence in my head.

That evening I told Timor. Although he took the news lightly, I could feel that my son wasn't acting normally. He slept in my bed for three nights in a row. That wasn't like him at all. Last night we had a rather interesting conversation.

When I tucked him in my bed, and was going to read him his favorite book, he said out of the blue, "You know Josh isn't allowed to sleep in his mom's bed anymore." Josh was his best friend. Josh's mom was divorced, but she remarried last year.

"Um, ... I think Josh is old enough to sleep in his own bed," I said unsure where this conversation was heading.

He shook his head, "Josh said it's because his stepdad sleeps in his mother's bed, there is no room for him."

Poor Josh, I thought, "It's not like that honey, I am sure Josh has a nice room, where he can sleep, and I bet his room is next to his mom's room." I knew Josh's mom, she's a sweet woman and a caring mother, I don't think she would neglect her son.

"Yes, but he said, while he was looking at them through the keyhole he saw…" He leaned closer and whispered in my ears what his friend saw. I was speechless for a moment, then he added, "When he told our teacher at school, she said it is wrong to look through the keyhole, and he shouldn't do that again."

"Your teacher is right; Josh shouldn't have done that. That wasn't nice. Besides, he shouldn't tell everyone about it." I gave him a "Don't you ever do that" look. Poor Josh's mom, I thought; sure she had no idea that the whole first grade knew what was going on in her bedroom.

I opened his book and wanted to distract him by reading, but before I could start he asked me, "Are you going to do like Josh's mom?"

"No," I answered quickly.

"Would I still be able to sleep in your bed?"

"You sure would," I gave him a reassuring smile, then I added, "Nothing is going to change, I promise."

"You're still going to sleep alone," he said, and I nodded.

"Why?" He asked.

"Why what?" I asked back.

"My friends at school say that moms and dads sleep in the same bed, this is how babies come," he explained to me.

"Um… I'll tell you a secret but don't tell everyone at school, okay," I looked at him.

He nodded and said "Okay."

"Well, Adam snores at night so I will sleep in a separate room," I said.

He grinned and asked, "Do I have to wear a suit at the wedding?"

"I am afraid so, yes," I confirmed.

He nodded and didn't argue. It seemed that the suit wasn't a real issue. At last, he opened the book so that I could read it for him.

After he fell asleep, I stayed up for a while, hoping that I was doing the right thing.

Chapter Six
Talia

This morning I met my sisters to help me choose my dress. This was the easy part; I wasn't wearing a wedding gown. I wanted something simple and elegant at the same time. I had an idea of how it should look in my head.

When I saw a crème cocktail dress, I knew it was the one. It was a sleeveless, knee-length dress. Its built-in bodice and straight cut skirt will give my figure the perfect shape. My sisters loved it when I tried it on, so I didn't look any further. I bought the dress and moved to the shoe department, where I found a pair of crème pumps that went perfectly with it; I bought them as well.

"Mission accomplished," I said and wanted to leave the store, but my older sister Olivia stopped me, "Wait! you still need to buy some sexy underwear."

"No one is going to see my underwear, come on let's put the shopping bags in the car and have an early lunch, I'm starving," I said and dragged her out of the store before she could object.

Tessa recommended a newly discovered Italian restaurant. The place was nice and cozy. After we took our seats at a rear table by the window, and a waiter took our orders, Olivia said again, "You should have bought new underwear."

I looked around, when I was sure that no one could hear us, I said, "What for? Adam won't see my underwear."

"He won't see it tomorrow, but he is going to see it soon," she said.

"No, he won't, we have a deal, remember," I insisted.

She shook her head and said, "This no sex rule is ridiculous, you won't be able to keep that one. I bet you won't last a week before you break it."

"No, Talia is stronger than that, I'd give her a month," Tessa corrected her.

"Thanks a lot for having so much faith in me," I said sarcastically.

"This has nothing to do with faith, but let's face the facts here. You're going to live together under the same roof for at least a year.

He is handsome, attractive and very hot, you'll be tempted," Olivia simply said.

She was right about one thing; Adam is attractive, no one can argue that. His face is well-defined with a sharp jaw and angular cheekbones. He has strong arched brows and eyelashes so thick, it should be illegal, and his eyes are deep and green. His dark brown thick hair and slightly dark complexion make him look dangerously handsome.

He isn't one of those rich men who looked like a fermented potato and hide their large bellies under their expensive suits and large bank accounts. He is tall and broad, if his suits hide anything, they would only hide his well-trained muscular body. In other words, Adam is gorgeous, but he isn't mine. I have to remember that.

"You two don't understand, Adam won't be around most of the time; he's very busy, and he travels a lot. We won't see each other that often. I am not going to get to know him. However, by the end of our marriage, I might be best friends with his assistant. Besides, he's not interested," I explained.

In the past four days, I spoke to Adam only once, and it was short and formal. However, I met his assistant twice and talked to her on the phone several times. We discussed the wedding plans and she helped me move my things to his house. She also gave me a detailed idea of our honeymoon, which in fact is a business trip to New York, where Adam is going to attend a few meetings.

Although I appreciated his assistant's help, the whole thing gave me an idea of how my life is going to be for the next twelve months.

Tessa interrupted my thoughts, when she said, "You have to accompany him on some of his business trips, you'll spend time alone together. Don't worry; he is going to be interested."

"I am not worried, I am only trying to tell you that we're going to stick to the rules," I told them and was hoping they would finally drop the subject. Before Olivia could argue, the waiter brought our food.

The food was excellent, and they were both distracted and left me alone for the rest of our meal.

On the drive home, I thought about my sisters' words, but I am not going to make the same mistake twice. I will not fall for Adam Grant. I am going to marry him tomorrow, but this marriage will remain a business deal and nothing more.

Chapter Seven
Adam

It was my wedding, as expected, everything was elegant and classy. We exchanged our vows and rings in front of all our guests, cut the cake, and had our first dance. I needed a few minutes to myself to sort out my thoughts, which wasn't possible with Talia by my side. I picked a distant table at the rear end of the garden and sat there to think.

My decision to marry Talia was impulsive, but it was the right one. I had to find a way to stop the damage that my former fiancé's photos and news were causing me.

The best way was to make a clean cut was by getting married. I was kept telling everyone we weren't getting back together as she claims. Now people won't connect her to me anymore; I made it clear to everyone that she was replaceable. Her actions won't embarrass me or harm my image anymore. *I did the right thing,* I kept telling myself the whole evening.

However, every time I see Talia, I think I got myself into a lot more trouble. She is different than all the women I've known before. I've always known what they wanted, and I was the one who decided how much to give. With her, I am not sure.

I can't tell if she is the person she is claiming to be, or if all this is part of a big show. The past few days I tried to avoid her; I let my assistant call her and arrange everything with her instead of doing it myself.

I wasn't that busy; I just wasn't sure how to deal with her. When she refused to hire a nanny for her son, I was alarmed. I thought she must have known my history with my mom and was pretending to be a devoted mom to score with me. So, I kept my distance.

However, that isn't going to work anymore; she's my wife now, and I won't be able to keep her at arm's length any longer. I've been watching her the whole evening; she is a loving mom, there is no doubt about that. I could tell from the way she looks and smiles at her son; her eyes are full of love and affection.

She has a lovely family; it doesn't take a genius to notice that they are close. Although they all have welcomed me with open arms into their family, they made it clear that this won't be the case if I ever hurt her. She won't get hurt if we stick to our plan, but I'm no longer sure I can do that.

I want to renegotiate our terms, this no sex rule, won't work for me. I realized this when I kissed her earlier. We were exchanging the rings, and the kiss was supposed to be a part of the show, it should have been brief and casual, but it wasn't.

When my lips touched hers, sparks flew in every direction, instead of keeping it short and small I pulled her closer and kissed her deeper and more passionately. A kiss like that was a beginning; it was a promise of much more to come.

Then came our dance. When I lead her to the dance floor, we were very close; our bodies almost touched. It was very hard to ignore the heat radiating between us. I was well aware of her warm body and her seductive scent.

I want more; I don't have any doubts about that. I can tell from the way she kissed me back and the way she was blushing during our dance; she wants more too. The problem is that I wasn't sure how she would interpret it. Women often mistake sex for love. I don't want her to get the wrong idea, this marriage is temporary, and it is going to stay that way.

I was debating the best approach to make her agree to my new terms when I heard my father asking, "Why is the groom sitting here all by himself?"

"Hi Dad, I'm only taking a break," I said.

"Grooms don't take a break, son. Do you have cold feet already?" He grinned.

"Why should I have cold feet? This is not real, remember," I reminded him.

He shook his head and said, "The way you kissed your bride earlier looked very real to me."

"Dad, it was part of the show. For the photos and the press; nothing serious," I told him.

"I like her though. She is different. If you let her, she would make you happy," he said.

"You don't even know her," I insisted.

"It doesn't take a genius to see that she is not like the others. You're a smart man; you'll know what you have to do," he said and gave me an encouraging smile.

"What do you mean?" I wanted to know.

He sighed and said, "Forget this ridiculous agreement, make it real. You don't want to live your life alone."

"What's wrong with that? You haven't remarried after mom left," I countered.

"Yes, but I had you, what do you have other than your money? You're thirty-four, what are you waiting for before you start a family and have kids of your own?"

When I didn't respond, he patted my shoulder and left.

My dad's words confused me a little, but he was wrong, even if Talia is different, she is still marrying me for my money. I can't forget about this agreement.

Marriage in my world is a contract, a business deal; it works as long as both parties agree to each other's terms and conditions. What I'm doing isn't new, people with money and power do it all the time, and I am one of them.

However, having a child won't be a bad idea. I could add it when we renegotiate. I thought about the new terms for a while, and they made perfect sense to me. I am going to discuss them with Talia, not tonight but soon. I have to choose the right moment to bring this up.

I took a look at my watch and realized that I'd been sitting here for almost half an hour. So, I rose up and went back to the party. Halfway to the house, I heard Timo calling, "Adam!"

"Timo, what are you doing here? Shouldn't you be in bed now?" I asked.

"I wanted to tell you goodnight before I go to sleep," he said with a smile.

"Goodnight, little champ," I said and caressed his hair.

I expected him to go inside, but instead, he looked at me and said, "Do you know why mom won't sleep with you?"

I was speechless; I didn't know how to respond to that. Fortunately, Timo didn't wait for my response, he just added, "Because you snore."

I didn't know what he was talking about, but I nodded anyway.

"I don't snore; I can sleep in mom's bed," he said proudly.

"Of course, you can," I said quickly.

Before he could say anything more, Talia came and rescued me. "Timo, what are you doing here? Granny is waiting for you upstairs," she told her son.

"I wanted to tell Adam goodnight," he said.

"Okay, but we don't want to keep Granny waiting. Please go up and change into your PJs. I'll come and tuck you in before I leave," she told him and gave him a warm smile.

He nodded and said, "Bye Adam." Without waiting for me to reply he ran to the house.

"A nice kid," I said and watched him running.

"Yeah, he's the best. I am lucky to have him," her eyes lit while she was watching her son go into the house.

"He gave me a tip about why you won't sleep with me," I told her.

Even though it was dark, I could see her blushing. I didn't give her a chance to respond, I closed the distance between us and added softly, "If snoring is your only problem, I don't snore."

When she raised her head to answer, her eyes were on the same level as my lips; the air was charged again. I could feel she wanted to kiss me. Before she could change her mind, I leaned in and kissed her slowly and softly. She pulled away, was blushing even more, "I… I'd better go check on Timo." She quickly left.

We are definitely going to renegotiate soon, and it won't be that hard, I thought and was pleased with myself.

Chapter Eight
Talia

What the Hell just happened?

He kissed me again. When he kissed me after we exchanged our vows and rings, I was prepared, I knew it was for the show. Of course, I wasn't expecting it to be that passionate, but I told myself he was trying to look convincing.

What just happened was something else, we were alone, he wasn't trying to prove anything to anybody.

I wasn't sure how I felt about that. We have chemistry; there is no doubt about that. I haven't reacted that way to anyone in a very long time. No, I haven't reacted that way ever, not even with my ex-husband.

Chemistry or not, you should be careful, this is a business deal, don't forget that, I kept reminding myself as I went upstairs to my old bedroom. When I entered the room, Timo was already in bed. His eyes lit and said, "I thought you left."

"How can I leave without kissing you goodbye?" I said and lay on the bed beside him.

"Are you leaving now?" He asked.

I nodded and said, "I'm going to miss you like crazy."

He smiled and said, "I'm going to miss you too, but Granny said you'd call us every day."

"I will, I promise. But you have to promise me you'll be a good boy and don't give Granny a hard time," I told him.

He didn't reply, he just nodded and cuddled up to me.

I kissed him and said, "I love you to the moon and back."

He rewarded me with a genuine smile before he started yawning.

"Goodnight baby, sweet dreams," I said and tucked him in.

"Night, mom," he said, his voice sleepy.

I kissed him again and rose up to leave. Before I reached the door, I heard him calling, "Mom!"

"Yes, honey," I stopped and looked at him.

"I like Adam" he said, before closing his eyes.

"I like him too," I murmured and left the room.

Downstairs, I found Adam waiting for me.

"Ready to leave?" He asked.

I smiled and nodded. We said our goodbyes to everyone and left.

The drive to his house wasn't long, and he drove in silence. He didn't say anything about our kiss, and I was grateful for that. I wasn't sure how to respond if he mentioned it.

When we arrived, it was late; the place was quiet. "Mrs. Smith must have retired for the night," he told me.

For a moment I was confused, I didn't know who Mrs. Smith was. "Mrs. Smith is my housekeeper, she takes care of everything here and also cooks for me. She has a separate apartment on the east wing. The guards are in the guest house in the garden," he explained.

When I nodded, he gave me the keys and said, "Welcome home."

I wasn't sure what to say, *this isn't my home,* was the first thing that came to my mind.

But I didn't want to sound rude. So, I smiled at him and just said, "Thank you."

"This is your home for the next twelve months," he said as if he was reading my mind.

"I'd better not get used to it, or it's going to be hard to move back to my old apartment," I said and took a few steps into the lounge. I looked around and took a seat on a nearby sofa.

"You won't need to go back there; you'll be able to afford something better," he reminded me and sat next to me.

I didn't answer, I only nodded. Adam was close; I could feel his eyes on me. I tried not to look at him and kept myself busy admiring the beautiful furniture.

"Do I make you nervous?" He suddenly asked.

"No," I said quickly. Though I wasn't looking at him, I knew he was grinning.

"Okay, maybe a little," I confessed a moment later when I turned to face him, he was smiling.

"You shouldn't be, you have to get used to my touch. I'm going to do that often." He told me, his eyes on my lips.

I knew what he was going to do, but I was faster this time. I rose up before he could kiss me again. I gave him an innocent smile and said, "I am okay with that, as long as it is for show."

"Good, because I won't appreciate it if you jump back every time I touch or kiss you. In New York, I am going to do a lot of that. There will be two business dinners and a gala that you have to attend with me." His tone was distant and professional.

"Don't worry, I know how to act in public," I said and tried to use the same tone he was using.

I could see he was upset. But what was he expecting? We had a deal, and we have to stick to it. I have to keep my distance, and he has to respect that.

"Fine, let me show you to your room, then." He rose up to walk me to my room. He noticed my surprise when we stopped at the master suite.

"You can't expect to stay in the other end of the house, you'll have your room, but we are sharing this suite," he grinned and opened the door.

The room was huge and had beautiful furniture. I could see my things were already there. When I came here a few days ago I left everything downstairs; I didn't come up here.

I wonder how many women slept in this bed, I thought when I looked at the bed.

For the second time, he read my thoughts and answered my unspoken question. "You're the first; I never bring women here, even my former fiancée didn't come here. We lived in the penthouse I own down town."

I didn't know what to make of this, but I was flattered. He didn't give me a chance to say anything, he just went on. "My driver is going to be here at eight in the morning to drive us to the airport. I have some work to do; I'll be in my office. I'll leave you to rest now, goodnight."

"Night," I said, but I wasn't sure he heard me. He left the room as soon as he ended his sentence.

This is going to be a long year.

Being Adam's wife won't be an easy job. I have to figure out the best way to deal with him, but not tonight. I looked at the massive bed in front of me and realized how exhausted I was. I quickly changed into my PJs and went straight to bed.

Chapter Nine
Adam

After I left Talia, I went to my office. I didn't lie when I said I had work to do; I have to go through some contracts before my meeting in New York. The problem was I couldn't concentrate.

All I could think about was Talia, sleeping in the room joined to mine. She was so close and yet so far. She noticed that I was upset when she jumped back before I could kiss her. I couldn't hide it. But she was the one who was sending me mixed signals here.

When I kissed her at her parents' house she was responsive; I could tell she wanted me as much as I wanted her. Maybe she wants more money; it's always about money, I thought. She isn't different from the others. Next time I'll make it clear to her that new terms mean new price.

Although I was satisfied with the conclusion I reached, I still couldn't focus on the papers in front of me. At last, I gave up and packed the contracts in my briefcase to review tomorrow on the plane.

I didn't want to go upstairs, Talia might still be awake. Instead, I went to the gym. I have a well-equipped gym in my house; I use it at least four days a week. Although I worked out this morning, tonight I need some physical activity to be able to sleep.

After running five miles on the treadmill, I finally went to sleep.

I woke up earlier the next morning; hearing movement from Talia's room at five thirty, half an hour later I heard her in the shower.

I needed all my willpower and self-discipline to stop myself from joining her. A few moments after I heard her door close, I rose up to shower and get ready too.

She was in the kitchen preparing breakfast and talking to someone on the phone. She heard me coming; turned around to face me and ended her call. I looked at my watch, it wasn't even seven o'clock. I frowned and asked, "Who are you calling that early?"

"Good morning to you too, I was talking to Timo," she said.

"Morning, I was surprised that's all, it's weekend, and it's not even seven," I explained.

"Timo is an early bird. It doesn't matter if it is school or holiday, weekdays or weekend, he never sleeps past six thirty." Her eyes lit up as they usually do when she talks about her son.

"So, are you an early riser too?" I wanted to know.

"Well I got used to it, but to be honest, I wouldn't mind sleeping in on the weekends. However, since Timo was born, it wasn't an option anymore," she said and smiled.

I drank my coffee in silence; then noticed that Talia was staring at my outfit and grinning. I took a look at my T-shirt to see if there was a stain or something and when I didn't find anything unusual, I looked at her and asked confused, "What's so funny?"

She shook her head and said, "Nothing, I just realized that this was the first time I've seen you wearing something other than a suit. I thought you sleep in one."

I took advantage of the situation, leaned closer and almost whispered, "If you're interested, I'd be happy to show you what I sleep in."

She almost choked in her coffee, I could see she was blushing, but she managed to say, "It's tempting, but I'll pass."

"Believe me, you'll be missing a lot," I shrugged.

She chose to ignore what I said, and asked, "What time is our plane?"

"Whenever we're ready; we are flying in my private jet," I told her.

"Of course, you won't fly like normal people," she said almost to herself, and before I could say anything she rose up. On her way out, she said. "Well, I'd better get ready, we don't want to keep your pilot waiting." I could hear the sarcasm in her voice, but I chose to ignore it. I went to my office and took what I needed from there.

An hour later we were on our way to the airport.

Chapter Ten
Talia

The flight to New York wasn't very long; only five hours. Adam's private jet was impressive. It was designed to be his home away from home. It has a dining room, office desk, and lounge area.

The five large, luxurious cabin zones were big enough to fit twelve passengers. When we were in the air, he showed me the large master suite at the back. It had a queen-size bed and a walk-in shower. "I didn't know that flying could be such fun," I said and sat on the bed to try it.

He closed the door and sat next to me, "If you let me I'll show you how much fun flying can be. I am more than willing and completely available," he whispered in my ear. When I didn't respond, he continued in a low voice, "I know you want me as much as I do. I can feel it. Why don't you give in to the moment?"

I opened my mouth to object. I wanted to sound sarcastic and make fun of his overconfidence, however, the instant I did, his mouth captured mine and I was lost. He possessed me with his hands, mouth, and tongue.

For the first time in years, my brain wasn't functioning, and I didn't want it to work, I wanted to let go and enjoy the ride. I didn't resist when Adam pressed me gently back to the bed. I pushed myself more tightly to him in response. He was kissing me, touching me, his mouth and hands were everywhere. He was smiling when I moaned as he opened the buttons of my blouse.

His soft kisses, his warm breath and his capable, strong hands they were magic, I was lost in the moment until he ruined everything.

"Twenty thousand more every month," he said between kisses.

At first, I didn't understand what he was saying, but his words alarmed me, my brain cells started to work, and I realized the meaning of his words. I quickly pulled back and began to button my blouse up.

He looked at me, confused by my sudden action, "What's wrong?"

"Nothing wrong, this was a mistake that's all," I said and tried to hold my tears.

Don't cry, don't cry, I kept telling myself. He was clueless; he didn't even notice what he did wrong.

"I thought you wanted this," he frowned.

"I did, but not anymore. Please, would you leave now? I'll join you in a minute." I jumped from the bed and opened the door for him. My tone was decisive, he couldn't argue. He rose up, buttoned his shirt and left the room.

I closed the door behind him and sat on the floor. I remained like this for a few minutes; I didn't know what to do or how to feel. He believes I'm a call girl, I thought. I was hurt, I was upset, and I was angry but mostly at myself.

I heard the little voice in the back of my head saying, *you did this to yourself.*
Finally, my anger took the upper hand, this was a mistake, and I am about to correct it.

I went to the bathroom, washed my face, straightened my clothes and went out to join him.

I could see that the hostess set the table and brought our lunch. Adam wasn't eating; he was waiting for me. I took a seat opposite him and made myself busy with the food in front of me. The food looked and smelled excellent, but I didn't taste anything, I was eating so that I don't have to look at him.

We ate in silence for a few more minutes then he finally broke the silence and said, "Listen, you misunderstood my words earlier."

Now I was furious; he didn't even want to apologize. "There was nothing to misunderstand; your words were crystal clear. Anyway, thanks a lot for your generous offer but I'd rather stick with our old terms," I said and gave him a fake smile.

"That isn't possible, we both know it. We have chemistry; I want you and you are attracted to me. I wanted to renegotiate our terms; I just chose the wrong moment," he shrugged.

I couldn't believe what I was hearing, "You just chose the wrong moment! You think that was all that you did wrong!" My voice was loud. Before he could say anything more, I went on, "Well, you're right about one thing though; we need to find new terms. It wasn't realistic to expect you to keep your pants on for a whole year. You can do whatever you want as long as you keep it discrete."

"What is that supposed to mean?" he wanted to know.

"It means you can have your affairs, I don't mind, just leave me out of this. And before you ask, I won't do the same if that is what is stopping you," I said, managing to stay calm this time.

"I don't accept that," he shook his head.

"We had an agreement, and you should respect it. As long as we are in public, I'll play my role as your loving wife. However, you have to keep your hands to yourself when we're alone." I said standing up and leaving the table.

I returned to my seat, turned my laptop on and tried to focus on my work for the rest of the flight. Adam saw me and did the same.

Chapter Eleven
Adam

Talia totally ignored me for the rest of the flight. She was busy with her work and didn't even glance at me. I didn't know what I did wrong, I was offering her more money.

What the hell was wrong with that?

After we landed, my driver was waiting for us. Talia was silent the whole time. As soon as we arrived at my penthouse, she locked herself in her room. I didn't like it, but I decided to give her time to calm down. I went to my office and did some work.

By the time I finished going through everything for my meeting on Monday, I felt hungry. I wanted to ask Talia out for dinner, but I knew she would decline. Instead, I ordered pizza, *one can never go wrong with pizza,* I thought. And I was right.

Talia came out of her room as soon as she smelled the food, I don't know if it was the pizza or she was just hungry. Anyway, we ate together. Although she tried her best to sound normal, I could feel she was still upset.

Why should I care if she's upset? She is working for me. I am paying her to be my wife. So, she is an employee nothing more.

I tried to analyze our situation, I did nothing wrong, the one who pays is the one who sets the rules. It's simple.

However, I couldn't tell why I cared. Maybe because I couldn't have her and I am not used to that. She said I could have any woman I want, but I want her, and I always gets what I want.

No one else will do, I get hard from just thinking about her. No woman has ever done that to me. Eventually, I will have her, she was melting in my hands a few hours ago, she wants me too. I am sure of that. All I have to do is to be patient and come up with another plan.

I took a long cold shower and had a good idea; I was going to call Timo, he was her soft spot. If I get him, I get her. I wasn't really proud of myself, using the boy to get his mother, but I couldn't think of anything better.

I called his grandma and asked her to put him through. She was concerned. First, she wanted to know if Talia was alright. I assured her that everything was great, and I only wanted to start a relationship with Timo. Although she sounded suspicious, she let me talk to him.

My initial plan was to chatter with him a little and make him like me so that I would score some points with his mom. But after we chatted for a few minutes, and he told me about his day with his friend Josh, I found myself telling him, "I need to ask you something buddy, I hope you can help me."

"Okay," I heard him saying on the other side.

"I wanted to know, what do you do when mom is mad at you?" I asked him, and I thought, *great now I am taking advice from some six-year-old kid.*

"Um… mom doesn't get mad at me," he said instantly, then he added, "Unless I did something really, really bad. Did you do something bad?"

"No, but she is upset with me, you know, grown-up stuff," I explained.

"Okay, when she's mad I draw her a picture and write down that I am sorry. I can write alone now, but in the past, Granny would help me. You know how to write, right?"

"Yeah, I don't need help with that," I said to him.

"I don't need help anymore," he said proudly.

"That's it, you just draw a picture and write you're sorry?" I wanted to know.

"Yeah, mom can't stay mad for a long time. After she sees my picture, she always smiles and gives me a kiss." Before I could respond he asked, "Do you want mom to kiss you, too?"

I want a lot more than that, I thought, but I didn't tell him that. Instead I said, "No, I only don't want her to be upset."

"Just say sorry but wait until she drinks her coffee first," he gave me a tip. I heard his grandma calling him to eat his supper. I realized that we've been talking for more than fifteen minutes. So, I quickly ended our call, telling him,

"Thanks, buddy, now go, Granny is waiting for you."

"Bye Adam," he said and hung up.

After I got off the phone with him, I felt so bad about myself. Timo was a great kid, and

I shouldn't use him to score a few points with Talia.

That was cheap, I thought and determined to keep Timo out of my plans for his mother in future. However, I still planned to make use of the tips he gave me.

I drew her a picture and wrote down *I am sorry*. I hung it on the fridge so that she could see it when she enters the kitchen. I sucked at drawing, but I guessed she wouldn't mind.

Next morning when I entered the kitchen, I found her sitting there drinking her coffee, she had my picture in her hands and was staring at it.

"Good morning, and thanks," She said as soon as she noticed me.

"Does this mean that we're on speaking terms again?" I asked.

She gave me a warm smile and nodded. *Timo was right; Talia can't stay mad for long,* I thought.

"I guess I'll have to thank Timo," I said. When she looked puzzled, I pointed at the picture and said, "It was his idea."

"You talked to him? When? He didn't tell me that," she was surprised.

"Well, I called him last night after dinner, I guess he didn't tell you because he thought it was men stuff," I grinned.

Her smile got brighter, she looked at the drawing in front of her and told me, "That's what he always does when he does something wrong, but I never really get mad at him."

"He said pretty much the same to me. However, he told me, you usually give him a kiss when he says sorry," I said waiting for her response.

"You're right, I guess I owe you a kiss then, but first you have to promise to keep your hands to yourself," she gave me a warning look.

"I promise, I won't touch you again. Not until you ask for it," I teased.

She shook her head and said, "Someone is so full of himself."

I didn't answer, I only grinned. Talia took a deep breath before she came closer; I could feel her eyes on my lips. I was waiting to feel her soft lips on mine again, but instead, she leaned and gave me a quick kiss on the cheek.

"That doesn't count," I complained.

"That's how I kiss Timo, and it's all you're getting," she said on her way out. She gave me an amused smile and just left.

I stayed where I was for a few more minutes after she left. I caught myself staring at her door like a teenager. Although her kiss wasn't intimate, we were making progress.

Soon she will give in, I thought.

Chapter Twelve
Talia

The look on Adam's face when I kissed him on the cheek was priceless. He wasn't expecting that, he wanted a real kiss, and to be honest, I longed for it too. But if I kissed him the way he wanted, we would have ended up finishing what we started on the plane yesterday. I wasn't ready for that yet.

I wasn't upset with him anymore, not after he apologized, but his words yesterday gave me a hint about how he felt and what he wanted, sex and nothing more.

What's wrong with that? I can't believe I am considering it; I don't even like sex.

That was true; Jeff, my ex-husband was my first. Throughout our marriage, our sex life was always about him. At first, I didn't mind, but after a while, I started to resent this part of our life, especially after I knew about the other women.

He was the one who told me, he claimed that it was all my fault; I couldn't satisfy him and I was never enough. I believed him; I thought I was one of those women who didn't enjoy sex, and I came to terms with that. After the divorce, I didn't want to repeat the experience. So, I cut men out of my life.

It wasn't hard; I had my son and my work; they were more than enough. I never longed for a man's touch. Not until recently, when Adam came into the picture. What I feel every time he touches me is new and confusing.

I need to think about this, and I can't do that when he's around. Although I hate shopping, I was grateful for the shopping tour that I have to do today. It would distract me and give me some time alone to sort my thoughts.

Once I showered and changed, I went to find Adam. He was in his office working and when he noticed my presence, he looked away from the screen in front of him and asked, "Ready?"

"Yeah," I nodded.

"Good, Robert will drive you," he said shortly.

I assumed Robert was his driver. "It's not necessary, I can take a cab."

"Robert will take you; he knows where to." He didn't give me a chance to argue, when

I didn't answer he told me, "Ask for a Ms. Elliot, she will be waiting for you and help you find what you need."

He took his credit card out of his wallet and said, "Use this, the store you're going to is very expensive, and you need to buy a few things for the events we have this week."

I shook my head, "I won't take your card, we have already discussed that, but I'll let Robert drive me and this Ms. Elliot help me. Happy now?"

"No, but I know how to choose my battles, and I won't win this one." He put his card back in his wallet.

"Good to know that you're a fair loser." I gave him a triumphant smile.

He shook his head, and in two steps he was standing before me, "I never lose, I am only saving my energy for the right battle, the one I want to win." He was so close I could feel the heat radiating from his body. I quickly took a step back and asked, "Is that a threat?"

He closed the distance between us again, his eyes on my lips, and I thought he was going to kiss me, but he didn't. Instead, he said, "It's a promise."

I didn't know whether I should feel intimidated or excited, but one thing was clear though: I was disappointed that he didn't kiss me. Before I could decide what to say, he told me, "You should leave now if you don't want to be late."

I nodded and quickly turned around and rushed out of the room. I was sure anyone could tell that I was blushing. On my way down, I was thankful for the private elevator; no one is going to see me like this.

Adam's driver, Robert, was waiting for me, when he saw me coming out of the lift he instantly hopped out of the car and opened the car door for me. I took my place in the back seat, and we drove in silence. The relatively short drive helped me cool off.

The store wasn't a massive department store as I assumed, it was rather a big boutique, which was well stocked with designer items. A nice lady welcomed me at the entrance and locked the door behind us. I gave her a questioning look, and she explained,

"I normally don't open on Sundays; I am Jade Elliot. It's nice to meet you, Mrs. Grant." She smiled and shook my hand.

I smiled back at her and said, "Talia please and I am sorry I interrupted your day off."

"It's okay; I own this place. I'll compensate myself later," she told me and smiled.

I liked her; she was an elegant lady in her early forties. From the look of the store, I could tell she has excellent taste.

Two hours later I had everything I needed; I bought a cocktail dress, three customs and the accessories that went with them. For the gala on Friday, Jade talked me into buying a daring evening dress.

Although I never wear red, I liked the way I looked in that dress; I felt sexy and confident. I realized that I was blushing when I imagined the look on Adam's face once he sees me in that dress. Jade must have noticed, she gave me a knowing smile and said, "This dress will have its desired effect, and you'll need these under it." She was holding a red sexy underwear set.

I wanted to tell her that Adam won't see them, but I quickly realized that I would be lying. It wasn't a question of whether he's going to see them it was a question of when he's going to see them.

Chapter Thirteen
Talia

After I left the store, I was in a good mood. I'd never spent that kind of money on clothes before, but I didn't feel bad about it. I loved every item I bought, and I wondered if Adam would like them too

I found myself thinking about Adam and our arrangement.

We need to set new rules, but they have to be my rules this time. I have to talk to Adam, and I will do it tonight.

On the way back to Adam's place, I had a plan. We were supposed to go out tonight, but I had other things in mind. I asked Robert to drop me at the nearest supermarket and picked up the ingredients I needed to prepare my famous lasagne.

Back at the penthouse, I put my shopping away in my room, the lasagne ingredients in the kitchen and I went to change. Twenty minutes later I was ready to start. The clock on the wall said three o'clock. I realized that I still had three hours before Adam returns, so I called my mom and Timo first.

After I hung up with my son, my mood was even better; I was smiling the whole time while preparing dinner. Once I put the lasagne in the oven and set the timer, I took a quick shower and changed into something more suggestive. I went for a black cocktail dress that I rarely wear and chose one of the crazily expensive underwear sets I bought earlier. I felt sexy and confident.

I was setting the table when I heard the front door close. A few moments later, Adam came in and when he saw the table, he frowned, "I thought we were going out tonight."

"Change of plans," I smiled at him and went on, "We are going to eat out every night for the rest of the week, I thought it would be a nice change if we ate here tonight."

"Yeah, but we could have ordered something, you didn't have to cook," he was surprised.

"I love to cook. I had time I didn't know what to do with," I shrugged.

That was true. I didn't want to go out again, although it was spring it was cold outside.

Adam stared at me for a moment, I couldn't tell what he was thinking, but I didn't give him a chance to brood any longer; I took a seat by the set-up table, "Let's eat before it gets cold."

He nodded and followed me after taking off his suit's jacket and tie. "How did you know that I love lasagne?"

"I didn't, but Timo loves my lasagne, and he is a real picky when it comes to food. I thought if he eats it you'd like it too," I told him.

"Well, you guessed right," he said and dished a large portion onto his plate.

I put a portion on my plate too; I was about to start eating when he said, "I didn't know you're a great cook, this tastes great."

I could tell he wasn't just paying me a compliment; he actually liked it.

"Glad you like it," I smiled.

We talked a little during our meal, I told him about my day and asked about his. His answers were short, but we kept the conversation going. By the time we finished eating, I emptied my glass of wine and poured myself another. I rarely drink alcohol; only on occasions, but tonight I needed a drink.

"We need to talk," I finally said what I was thinking the whole time.

"What about?" Adam asked amused.

He wasn't going to make this easy for me, I thought, "You know what about."

"No, I don't," he grinned.

I took a deep breath and told him, "About our arrangement."

"What about it?" he frowned.

I couldn't believe he was doing this to me; he wanted me to spell the words out.

"Fine, you were right, I am attracted to you too. I want to finish what we started yesterday." I took a large sip of my wine and went on, "No feelings, just sex, but with no extra money and no expensive gifts." Without waiting for his response, I left the table and took a few steps to face the massive window in the room. I didn't turn around, but I felt him right behind me. He turned me to face him, and looked me in the eye, "Are you sure?"

"I am sure," I nodded.

Adam hesitated for only a fraction of a second before he wrapped me in his strong arms and pressed his lips against mine. He tasted like wine, the scent of his expensive cologne was spicy and masculine, and his kiss was passionate and demanding. I knew I was risking my heart but after lying dormant for so long, having a man as powerful as Adam Grant devouring me wasn't something I wanted to resist.

Not anymore.

I opened my mouth to welcome his tongue. Adam ran a hand down my back and back up to touch my hair. He growled and pushed both hands into it. Without letting go of my hair, he held my face, and his gaze finally met my eyes. "I've never wanted a woman as much as I want you."

I didn't know what to say after this confession, but he didn't give me time to respond. He squeezed his lips against mine in desperation. When I let one hand fall to his hip, the other to his butt, Adam pressed me against the massive window and gathered my hands in his. He lifted them above my head and leaned into me. He was trying to slow this down by keeping me from touching him. It was frustrating and erotic.

Though we were both still fully clothed, I could feel the extent of his desire pressed on my belly, close but not close enough. He went on kissing me, hot, desperate kisses that left me completely breathless.

Adam was still restraining my hands, so I ran one leg up to him.

He pulled back. "If you keep touching me like this, I am going to take you right here, with all of New York watching."

I turned my head and caught the lights behind me. "Then let's find a proper bed," I suggested and then asked. "Your bed, or mine?"

One moment I was bound to the window, the next I was in his arms. "Mine's closer." He laid me on the white sheets. I welcomed him back into my arms and continued our kiss. The weight of him and his strength made me giddy. I pulled his shirt out of his slacks.

When my fingers met his bare skin, Adam moaned. I couldn't believe that I could make him lose control. The moment my dress came off, Adam froze in his place, "God, Talia.

What are you wearing?" His reaction to my lingerie was worth every cent I'd spent on it.

After a few moments Adam stopped staring and leaned forward to touch me everywhere, I tugged at his shirt, and it was on the floor with my dress. I knew Adam filled out a suit, but under it was something worth looking at. Everything about him radiates confidence and strength. He left the bed to shack his slacks, a few seconds later he was only in his boxer shorts.

He cupped my breasts with his hands, before moving back to unhook my bra. Adam replaced his hands with his mouth. I never felt so entirely ready to accept a man into my body, I never felt this cherished.

Adam took his time; he wasn't merely trying to get inside me, like my ex-husband used to do. I quickly pushed the memories from my mind and leaned back against the pillows to enjoy the feel of him.

I clenched the sheets in my fists when Adam touched my most needy parts. I was thinking I couldn't take it anymore when I heard him tearing the condom wrapper. Once he rolled the condom on, he was inside me and moving, slowly at first and then faster.

I clung to him while my body trembled. Adam followed me a second later with a growl. I waited a few minutes for my mind to process what just happened, I realized I just had my first orgasm, no, I had two of them if I wanted to be accurate. I felt incredible. From the smile on Adam's face, I could tell he was pleased too.

The weight of Adam's body pressed me into the bed, the sound of his breath was as rough and irregular as mine. I stretched my leg and ran down the back of his. I couldn't stop smiling.

How could this be possible, I never thought sex could feel so good. I've read about it, but I didn't believe that I would ever experience it. Not after what I went through with my ex-husband. I quickly pushed away the memories and focused on the sense of Adam who was still buried inside my body.

"That was..."

"Spectacular," he finished my sentence and rolled off me, so we laid side by side, dazed and entirely sated.

I wanted to ask him if it was really good for him, but my own uncertainty stopped me. Adam had a lot of lovers, from the photos I've seen, they were gorgeous. How could I compete with any of them?

Adam interrupted my thoughts, "What are you thinking?"

I didn't want to sound like a needy, emotional moron, but I was dying to know how he felt. "Was it… was it really good for you too?"

"What kind of question is that? Didn't you feel how well we fit together?" he asked, and I could see that he was surprised by my question.

Adam's astonished look made me blush. I regretted asking. He must have noticed my embarrassment because he gently lifted my chin so I could look into his eyes. "It was perfect, you are perfect. More passionate than I ever fancied."

I turned so that my legs were wrapped around his hips; my breasts touching his muscular chest. Our lips were so close I could still taste him. The look in his eyes was so intense; for a moment I felt a connection there. I was sure Adam felt it too.

He didn't give me a chance to say anything though. All of a sudden, he freed himself from my embrace and left the bed. I was confused when I saw him disappearing into his walk-in closet. A minute later he came out wearing a flannel pajama bottom and a white t-shirt. "Where are you going?" I asked before he could leave the room. I didn't understand his sudden change in mood.

"I still have some work to do," he said shortly. "You can sleep here, I'll sleep in the guest room."

I quickly jumped to my feet and gathered my things, "Thanks, but I'll sleep in mine." I was about to leave the room, but Adam stopped me and took me in his strong arms. He nibbled and kissed his way around my lips, neck and jaw, suddenly his attitude didn't suck. When I pulled away to breathe, his gaze met mine, "What we've just had was incredible, but I need my space. I hope you're fine with that."

I didn't answer; I just nodded and kissed him gently on the cheek. "Goodnight," I whispered before I left the room.

Alone in my bed, I tried to sort out my thoughts. Adam was right to need his space; I needed my own room too. I reminded myself that our marriage was temporary, but still, I could enjoy the time we have together. I would have an affair with my husband. I couldn't have said no to this.

I smiled as I realized that I'd have access to his incredible body and sexual talents for an entire year.

I should focus on that and not on what's going to happen a year from now.

I was satisfied with this conclusion. I feel asleep.

Chapter Fourteen
Adam

I didn't like the pain in Talia's eyes as I suddenly left the bed. But I couldn't stay, not after what I shared with her. I've never experienced anything like this before. I knew I was going to have her, but this was more than I could have ever wanted. I didn't expect her to be that passionate. When I pushed myself into her wet core, I felt like I was home.

The moaning noise she made as I was buried deep inside her tight body blew up my ego. I could feel her hot fast breaths as her hips started to move. It was amazing.

Although I never left a woman unsatisfied before, I never felt the urge to make a woman twist with lust. However, tonight I wanted to make Talia quiver with pleasure, pleasure that only I would bring her. I held back my own release and waited for her to fall from the cliff. She cried out my name as she did, only then I let go and followed her into heaven.

When I looked into her eyes I saw something more than lust; I saw affection and love. It scared me; I had to run. I lied about having work to do. I just wanted to escape.

I never spend the night with a woman in the same bed, I usually put my clothes back on and leave as soon as I can. It was one of my rules. Tonight though, I wanted to break this rule, I longed for Talia's warm body in my bed, under me, over me and wrapped around me. I wasn't lying when I told her that I never wanted a woman the way I wanted her. That was why I panicked so much and had to leave.

I never felt this way before not even with Sharon, my first love, the one who shredded my heart and was the main reason for my trust issues. The moment I found myself thinking about Sharon and what she did, I quickly shook off the bad memories.

One can't change the past, I told myself. *Unfortunately, one can't forget it either.* My past is still dictating my future.

Although I craved Talia's closeness, it was better to keep things as simple as possible. When I left my office, I wasn't brooding anymore. I told myself that Talia was mine for a year and a year was long enough.

In the morning, the smell of freshly brewed coffee drifted into my room and led me to the kitchen.

I entered the kitchen and took a seat at the kitchen counter. I found Talia speaking to someone on the phone while she was preparing breakfast. When she saw me, she gave me a warm smile and filled the plate in front of me with a serving of scrambled eggs and crispy slices of bacon. Then she placed a small amount on her plate.

A few moments later I heard her saying, "Bye honey, I love you too." I smiled and asked although I knew the answer, "Were you speaking to Timo?"

"Yeah, I wanted to call him before he goes to school," she explained and brought her plate and took a seat next to me.

"Is he going to have a problem with our new rules?" I wanted to know how things were going to be when we return to Seattle.

"What do you mean?" she frowned.

"I mean, would I be able to do that?" I pulled her to me and kissed her slowly and softly, she opened to me, and I deepened our kiss. Before the kiss could lead to something more, she pulled away and said,

"Um, about that, Timo is not used to seeing me do this."

"Do what?" I looked at her confused, "Kiss a man?"

"Yeah," she nodded.

"And how did your former boyfriends deal with that?" I thought she was joking.

"No one had to deal with anything; I haven't had any relationships since my divorce," she said.

I didn't quite understand what she was saying, so I asked, "You mean nothing serious, but you surely had flings and short-term affairs."

"No, can we eat now?" she said and looked down at the food on her plate.

I was shocked at her confession, I wanted to pursue it further, but I got her hint, she didn't want to talk about it.

We ate in silence for a few minutes, I could feel she was tense, and I hated to see her like this. So, I broke our silence by saying, "You know you're the first woman to make me breakfast."

"How about Mrs. Smith, isn't it her job to make you breakfast?" she countered.

As my housekeeper, Mrs. Smith made breakfast almost every morning, but I didn't mean it that way, and she knew it.

"Mrs. Smith doesn't count; I don't sleep with her," I countered back.

"It's your fault then, you don't let them," she said and smiled. When I didn't respond, she added, "Judging from your performance last night, I am sure lots of women would love to make you breakfast the morning after."

"Is that so?" I grinned.

She blushed and moved quickly to put the empty dishes in the dishwasher.

I followed her and blocked her way. When she was close enough, I kissed the sensitive skin of her neck and whispered, "I can perform even better after this breakfast."

Before she could object, I showed her how good, on the kitchen counter.

*****

The few days that followed were too busy, but I was in an excellent mood. Talia's closeness was refreshing; I liked spending time with her. I never had the urge to know a woman outside the bedroom, but I wanted to know her. I've only scratched the surface, and I already liked what I saw.

When my dad came to see me earlier today, he noticed my good mood. He repeated what he had told me at the wedding. He wanted me to forget about the arrangement I had with Talia and make things real. But I can't do that; I can't just drop my guard.

Although I decided that it was too soon to follow my dad's advice, his words were the only thing that I could think about, and they gave me a headache. After a while, when I realized that it was impossible to get any work done, I called it a day and went home.

Talia was in the living room working on her laptop when she noticed my presence, she put her computer to the side and asked concerned, "You're home early, is there something wrong?"

"Just a headache, nothing serious," I said and took my place on the couch next to her.

She came closer and gave me a light kiss.

"Let's cancel our dinner reservation and stay at home tonight," she suggested.

"But won't you be mad?" I looked at her. "We've been going out with clients almost every night; tonight was supposed to be just the two of us."

"It's still going to be just the two of us. We can order in, or I can fix us some light dinner," she gave me a warm smile.

"Any other woman would be disappointed and upset right now." I studied her for a moment to make sure that she wasn't upset.

She shook her head, "I am not one of those women."

On her way to the kitchen, she gave me a warm smile and suggested, "Why don't you take a shower and change, while I figure out what to do about dinner."

She was right; Talia wasn't like anybody I knew.

Chapter Fifteen
Talia

I was surprised when Richard, Adam's father called this morning and asked me to meet him. I knew that he arrived in New York yesterday; he had some business to do here. I was curious because I am supposed to meet him at the gala tonight.

What could be that urgent? I wondered on the way to his hotel.

I noticed Richard the moment I entered the hotel lobby. Even if I hadn't seen him before, I would have recognized him. The resemblance between him and Adam isn't something anyone can overlook; he is Adam in thirty years.

When he saw me, he quickly approached and said with a smile, "Here comes my favorite daughter-in-law."

"I am your only daughter-in-law," I countered.

"Well, that makes you my favorite," he countered back and led me out of the hotel to one of the cafes along the main street.

"They make a good pie here. I am having apple pie," I heard him saying after we took our seats on a back table by the window.

"Just coffee for me," I said to the waitress who was waiting to take our orders.

I was starting to get nervous, I had no clue why I was here, and I didn't like it. However, I didn't have to wait long. After the waitress left, Richard started talking, "You must be wondering why I wanted to see you."

"Actually, I do," I curtly confirmed.

"I want to talk to you about the arrangement you have with my son," he said and looked me in the eyes.

"Sorry, but I don't know what you are talking about," I wasn't sure how much he knew.

"Adam told me everything, and I don't like it," he said.

"Um… but I still don't know why this is any of your business, Adam isn't a child anymore," I said annoyed.

"You have a son too, Timo, right?" He didn't wait for my answer, he went on, "Won't you interfere to make him make the right choice?"

“Yes, but Timo is six, and I am responsible for him, Adam is a grown-up man. He is responsible for his own choices.” I didn't like my son being dragged into this conversation.

“Why are you getting so defensive? I am on your side here.” I looked at him confused, so he explained, “I think you’re the right one for my son, I want you to keep him.”

“This is ridiculous, I’ve only known your son for two weeks, how can you be sure I am the one for him?”

“I know my son; I haven't seen him this happy or this confused before. Yesterday he was grinning like a teenager who had sex for the first time.”

When I blushed, he continued, "I think you have feelings for him too."

“Even if you were right, don’t you think Adam has to want the same thing too?” I asked.

“I am sure he does, but he doesn’t want to admit it yet,” he said as the waitress brought the pie and coffee.

I added some cream to my coffee and thought about his words.

"All I am asking is that you hear me out, I want you to understand where Adam's trust issues came from."

When I nodded, he started to talk. First, he told me about Adam's relationship with his mother and how she left when he was just a little boy and didn't contact them for years.

I didn't interrupt him, so he kept going, "He's never forgiven her, but he helps her out every time she needs money."

I didn't know how to respond to that, so I just gave him a sympathetic look.

"Although his mother's desertion hurt him a lot, she isn't the only reason he mistrusts women."

"He was in college when he met someone; he was crazy about her. When she got pregnant, he was over the moon. He wanted to drop out of college and come work for me so that they can get married. However, when he proposed to her, she let him down and told him that she had already taken care of the pregnancy."

"Oh," that was all I could say.

"They fought, and she told him that the baby wasn't his. He was devastated of course and buried himself in his studies and then his work. He never had a real relationship again, until you came."

"I can't call our marriage a real relationship," I quickly corrected him.

"No, but you can make it real if you want," he said and gave me a warm smile.

"It takes two for a relationship to work. Adam has to want the real thing too," I told him.

"Give him time and be patient, that is all I am asking."

I thought about his request for a moment and then nodded, "I can do that."

"Good, I'll leave you to get ready for the gala tonight then."

The whole day I thought about nothing but what Richard had told me.

At the gala, Adam didn't leave my side. I caught him few times staring at me when he thought I wasn't looking.

"This dress is killing me. You look like Christmas tonight," he said while we were dancing.

"Wait till you see what I'm wearing under it," I gave him a cocky smile.

"Are you trying to seduce me, Mrs. Grant?" He cocked his head slightly.

"Maybe I am."

"You're certainly doing a good job. I am not sure I can last any longer," he said and pulled me closer so I can feel his excitement pressed on my belly.

Heated from his touch, his words and his hungry gaze, I looked at him, "Don't you think we've been here for too long?"

Without breaking our eye contact, Adam took his phone out of his pocket, called his driver and told him to bring the car to the front door.

In less than two minutes we were sitting in the back seat. I turned toward him, and he kissed me until every inch of my body was on fire. I didn't know if it was the kiss, the champagne, or my newly discovered sexual appetite. But I knew only one thing: *if I don't have him now I might just blow apart.*

I wasn't sure how it happened, but I was on top of him and pulling him to me. I gasped as he yanked my thin dress down to my waist.

His mouth, his hands, his scent were everything I so desperately needed. I wanted the thrust of him, hard and strong more than I wanted to breathe.

"Yes. Yes," I screamed as the tidal wave surged over me at last. I felt the heat, the pleasure and the spikes of madness as Adam's hard hands touched my flesh and his hungry mouth was on my breast.

Suddenly my hands were tugging on his belt; my mouth found his as I shoved his slacks down and closed my hands around him. We took each other in a kind of madness, all tempo and desperation breaking on pure pleasure.

I finally clung to him while the glory of those aftershocks trembled and shook.

When my mind was able to work again, I heard a little voice inside my head.

Adam is mine at least for the next twelve months.

Chapter Sixteen
Talia

It was the week before Thanksgiving. My life had changed since we came back from New York. Adam was right; our marriage generated a lot of publicity; it made the headlines in almost all newspapers. For months our pictures were on the cover of the major magazines. The press didn't connect him to his former fiancée anymore.

Adam gained what he wanted from our marriage, his stock surged as the shareholders renewed confidence in him. But he wasn't the only one to win from the publicity; I profited greatly too.

Shortly after we returned, I started attracting new clients. Most of them wanted to use my agency because I was Adam Grant's wife.

When I made it clear that they won't gain anything from my relationship with Adam, some of them withdrew their offers, but still, a few of them chose to stay and used my services.

Those who stayed were fond of my work and brought me more clients. With all the new orders I needed to expand. Six months ago, I hired an assistant, two more designers and rented three office rooms on the fifth floor in the same building as Adam's company. It was logical because Adam owned the building and he made me a good deal.

Now we work in the same building, we sometimes go out together for lunch, but mostly I bring food, and we eat his office. Eating is not the only thing we do here; we usually work up an appetite first. We've had sex everywhere in his office; on his desk, on the couch, even on the floor.

His employees noticed of course what we do in our lunch break. Last week I heard two of them talking in the ladies' room, they didn't know I was in. They called it Adam's sex break. When they saw me, they were mortified that I heard them, but I wasn't. I looked them in the eyes and gave them an amused smile. That was the new me. The old me would have left red-faced and avoided everyone for days.

I liked the new version of myself better. I became more confident and self-assured. Adam was solely responsible for this change. With him I feel sexy, wanted and attractive. I never felt this way before. I believed my ex-husband's words - he used to tell me that I was dull, boring and average in every way.

Although I had been divorced for years, his words were always ringing in my ears. Adam made them stop; I now hear his voice instead. I smiled at the thought of his voice and the dirty words he whispers in my ear.

Yesterday he came to my office before I could go up to him. He said that we needed to christen my office. For a moment I didn't understand what he meant, then he locked the door and gave me a wolfish smile.

I shook my head when I realized what he was about to do, "No way, my assistant could hear us."

"Mine hears us all the time." He came closer and smothered my protest with a ravenous kiss. Before I knew it, he pressed me against the door. He yanked up my skirt and slid his palm between my legs. "I am going to have you right here, against this door. I am going to watch you come first."

I had to grasp his shoulder as my knees trembled. His eyes, fiercely green, captured mine when my body exploded.

I was moaning when I heard him saying, "Tell me you want me."

I moaned again.

"Tell me you want this."

"Yes. God. Yes," I said and quickly lifted my leg to hook around his waist. His mouth toned down my cry of release as he thrust into me hard and deep.

When I finally came to my senses and was able to open my eyes, I found him staring into mine. They weren't only full of affection, but there was something more, but I couldn't put my finger on it.

When he smiled, I said, "Now we've officially christened my office." I looked around and smiled, "But I don't know how I am going to work here and not think about this."

"That was the plan," he gave me a broad smile, and tucked his shirt back into his slacks. Before he left, Adam kissed me one more time and said, "I want you to think about me every time you set foot into your office."

His plan worked. I was sitting there all morning thinking about nothing else. Good thing that I am meeting my sisters this afternoon. Tessa and I are going to help Olivia move her stuff to her new apartment.

I looked at my watch and decided that I'd better get going since getting any work done was hopeless. *Helping Liv will distract me,* I thought.

On the drive to Liv's old house, I was thinking about her and her divorce. I felt terrible that I wasn't there for her the past few months. But I was busy with everything going on in my life, and she drowned herself in work. She wasn't ready to talk about it.

Although I was sure that she was better off without Peter she was still hurting. They were married for five years and were living together for two years before that.

From the little she told us, I figured out that she saw this coming. She suspected that Peter was having an affair for months before she caught him with his pants down, in his office, doing it with one of his clients. The next day she filed for divorce. That was seven months ago and her divorce was finalized last week.

Even though she had a good lawyer, Peter took their house in the divorce settlement. He was one of the best divorce attorneys in Seattle and knew all kind of tricks. Besides, he never played fair. But Liv didn't mind losing the house; she said that she couldn't live there any longer and she needed a fresh start.

Will I be able to start over after my divorce too?

Suddenly my heart ached at the thought of my divorce. It was inevitable, however. My time with Adam was limited and I knew this from the start - I can't complain now, but I hadn't planned to fall for him.

Our arrangement planned for everything…except falling in love.

Chapter Seventeen
Talia

When I arrived at Olivia's old house, I only found Tessa's car there. I parked my car behind hers and went in to see how I could help.

Tessa was labeling the boxes. "Hey, you're late." I looked at my watch, I wasn't late. "Stop looking at your watch and give me a hand loading these boxes into my car."

"Where is Liv?" I asked as I carried one of the boxes.

"She finished loading her car and left for her apartment. She is waiting for us there," Tessa explained.

We worked together in silence for a while. When we were almost done, I asked again, "How is Liv doing?"

"You know Liv; she is good at hiding her feelings. But she is going to get over him," she shrugged.

"You never liked him," I observed.

"He wasn't your favorite either."

I looked at her for a moment and then said, "He made a move on you, didn't he?"

"Yeah, right after Seth's death. How did you know, I never told anybody?" She said, and her eyes were full of tears. Although Seth, her fiancé died almost three years ago, she still gets teary eyed when she mentions his name.

I patted her shoulder and said, "Because he made a move on me too."

"What? When?" She couldn't believe it.

"Right after my divorce. I guess Peter thought the three of us were a package deal. Buy one get two for free," I joked.

Tessa laughed, and I was about to carry another box to my car when she stopped me, "Wait a minute, right after your divorce, they weren't even married then. They had just moved in together." She did the math. "Why haven't you told Liv?"

"Liv was crazy about him, and she had a rough time after she broke up with Jason. I didn't want to hurt her," I simply said.

"Speaking of Jason, are you going to see him next week?"

Tessa nodded, "You know I have to spend Thanksgiving with the Hamiltons."

I honestly didn't know why, but I didn't tell her that so, I didn't comment, I only smiled at her, and we worked in silence.

Tessa and Seth used to spend Thanksgivings with his family and Christmas with hers. After he died, Tessa kept up their tradition, which means she has to see Jason and Aron, Seth's older brothers.

They all studied at Harvard together; the Hamilton brothers, Olivia and Tessa. Jason and Aron didn't study medicine, and they were a few years older than Seth and my sisters. For a while, it was the Hamilton boys and the Jones girls. Unlike Seth and Tessa, things didn't work out with Jason and Liv. Aron was a mystery though; he had nothing against Liv, but he never liked Tessa.

Tessa interrupted my thoughts, "These are the last boxes, let's put them in the car and drive straight to Liv."

Four hours later, we had unpacked most of the boxes. We finished the ones that belonged in the kitchen, the living room, and Liv's bedroom first. Liv told us that was enough for now; she was going to do the rest whenever she had time.

After we completed our mission, Tessa and I sat exhausted in the living room and waited for Liv who went to open the door for the pizza man. Two minutes later she came back with the Pizza. We chatted about various things as we ate. Then Olivia shot me a curious look and said, "I want to know what's going on with you and Adam. *Really* going on, with details."

"You are the one who supposed to be on the spot, not me," I tried to redirect the conversation.

"Nothing is going on in my life; I cried my eyes dry the past few months. It still hurts of course, but I am getting better," she shrugged, "Now it's your turn, what's going on?"

"Come on, Tal, spill. I am dying to know too," Tessa joined her.

"You know what's going on. Adam and I still have this arrangement. That includes sex now. Would you like some details about our sexual adventures?"

"I would, but we will leave that for our next girl night," Tessa suggested. "One that includes lots of wine and more Pizza."

"What do you want to know?"

"The obvious, how do you feel about him?" Liv said, and Tessa nodded.

I looked at them. They were both waiting with anticipation, "Fine. The simple answer is that I don't know. I like Adam, I enjoy our time together. He's interesting and smart. When he forgets about his billions, he can be really fun. He's great with Timo and Timo adores him." I took a deep breath before I continued, "Timo never had a father figure before, and Adam filled this gap. I hope the two of them stay close after the divorce."

"When are you going to tell him?" Tessa asked.

I looked at her confused, "Tell him what?"

"That you love him," It was Liv who answered.

"Who said I love him? I didn't say that."

"Honey, it's written all over your face. You're in too deep," Liv observed.

"He's into you, too. Adam can't keep his hands off you," Tessa told me.

"Yeah, but it's just sex, we don't even sleep in the same bed," I argued.

"No, it's not, and you know it," Liv challenged.

"Okay, maybe I do love him. But it's not enough. Even if Adam has some feelings for me, they aren't sufficient. He never speaks about anything more than what we have now," I told them.

"So, what are you going to do now?" Tessa wanted to know.

"There is nothing I can do. If I tell Adam that I love him, I might lose him. I don't want that. So, I am going to enjoy the time that we have left," I gave them a weak smile.

"He won't let you go. He's in deep, but he doesn't recognize how deep yet. Give him time and be patient," Tessa gave me a reassuring smile.

Her words reminded me of the advice Richard gave me when I met him in New York. *Time and patience. Unfortunately, I don't have much of those.*

Chapter Eighteen
Adam

Talia was spending the night with her sisters, they have been planning it for weeks and every time something came up. Tonight finally, all three of them had time. I told her she should go and have some fun with her sisters.

She hasn't been herself lately; every time I ask her what's wrong, she says work. But I know it has nothing to do with work, something is bothering her.

I haven't been myself for a while either. However, I know the reason. Our arrangement is going to end in less than two months. I don't know what to do about that. I am not ready to give Talia up yet.

The past ten months were the best of my life. I never lived with a woman before, and I didn't think that I would like it. But Talia wasn't like any other woman; she was easy to live with. I like coming home to her.

Although sex wasn't part of our deal, the moment my lips met hers, I knew that things were about to change and they did. However, it was supposed to be just sex, but the more I got to know her, the more it wasn't just sex.

I still couldn't define my feelings for Talia, but they were there. I was sure she felt something for me too. I could see it in her eyes when they gazed at me like I was the last chocolate cake on earth as I made love to her.

We crave each other's closeness, yet we never sleep in the same bed. I know that Talia longs to change that but I am not ready that kind of intimacy yet.

When I offered her this arrangement, I thought a year would be long enough. It never occurred to me that I would want more, but would she agree if I asked her to extend our arrangement a little longer? She never asked me about what would happen next, and lately, she was keeping her distance. *Maybe she doesn't feel the same way. What if she wants to go through with the divorce as planned?*

I panicked at the thought of that. Talia was only gone for the night, and I missed her already. Then I thought about Timo, and I couldn't picture my life without him either. We became very close to each other; I love the boy. He is a great kid, smart and always cheerful.

Talia did an excellent job with him was my thought when I heard him calling, "Adam, I'm ready."

"I'll be right up champ," I shouted so he could hear me.

Talia wanted to drive him to her parents on her way so that he could spend the night with them, but I told her there was no need and that the two of us were going to have a guys' night.

Timo was thrilled by the idea; he didn't give his mom a chance to say no. We've a great time so far; we played video games together and ate our dinner. I went down to take a break and drink a cup of coffee as he got himself ready for bed.

When I went to his room, Timo has already changed into his PJs and was waiting for me. He didn't have his book ready though.

"Where is your book buddy?"

"I don't want you to read me tonight, can we just talk instead?"

I was used to this introduction by now. It meant that we were about to have a Josh episode. Josh episodes were usually interesting, but sometimes they were embarrassing as hell.

"Okay, what's on your mind, champ? Do you have a girl problem at school?" I smiled and sat on the bed beside him.

Timo giggled and shook his head, "I am too young for that."

"You're almost seven, man, and still no girlfriend?" I looked him in the eyes, and he grinned. "No."

"If we're not going to talk about girls, what then?" I tried to sound serious.

"Babies," he said quickly.

I didn't expect that. I didn't know how parents respond to these kinds of topics and I wasn't sure what Talia would want me to say. "Um…what about them?"

"Josh is going to have a baby. I want one too."

"Josh is having a baby, isn't he too young for that?" I tried to joke.

"Not him, his mom is having a baby, and he is going to be a big brother. He brags about it all the time. I want to be a big brother too," he explained.

"You want a baby so that you can brag about it too?" I teased.

"No, but I want a baby brother, Josh is having a brother," he looked at me.

"What if you have a baby sister?" I was trying to discourage him.

"I'd rather have a brother, but a sister is fine too," he said and didn't give me a chance to respond, "Josh said, I should ask you for one."

"Um… you know moms are the ones who have babies, I think you should ask your mom." Now Talia can deal with this, I thought.

"Yes, but I saw the two of you kissing, and Josh's parents do this too, you know this is how babies come."

I nodded, and I was hoping he would drop the subject, but he said something that surprised me and filled my heart with joy at the same time, "If we have a new baby, you can be my dad too."

"Would you like that? Would you like me to be your dad?" I asked cautiously.

He nodded, "If…if it's okay with you?" I could see he was blushing.

I gently lifted his chin and looked into his eyes, "Nothing would make me happier or prouder."

He gave me a genuine smile, and I hugged him. "Now it's time for bed; we don't want mom to call and find you still up."

"Okay, goodnight dad."

"Goodnight champ." I turned off the light and left his room. I was happy and touched.

Timo has just called me, dad. Maybe that's it; we could have a baby. That way we can extend our marriage for another year or maybe two. I guess two would be enough.

I wanted to share this with Talia, I picked up my phone and called her.

A moment later I heard the phone ringing; the sound came from Talia's room. I frowned and went in. Her phone was lying there on her perfectly made bed. She must have forgotten it, I thought. It was strange though; Talia never forgets her phone.

I was about to leave the room when something caught my attention. I took a good look at it and froze in my place.

Talia is pregnant. Why hasn't she told me? What if she doesn't want the baby?

I shook my head, "No, Talia won't do that." I assured myself, but I needed to act quickly, I didn't want to take any chances.

I am not going to lose this baby too.

I grabbed my phone, called my lawyer and told him to send me a new prenup contract.

Late that night the contract was in my hands. It was a generous one and covered everything.

After I read it one more time, I was satisfied. Talia would agree to this, I was sure.

Chapter Nineteen
Talia

The whole drive to Liv's, I was in shock. How could this happen? We were careful. When I decided to take the pregnancy test because my period was late, I was only taking it to rule out pregnancy. I took the test three times; I am definitely pregnant.

What am I going to do? Adam finally trusted me. He hadn't told me that he loved me yet, but he didn't have to say the words. I could see them in his eyes and feel them in his touch. The past few weeks turned our relationship into something more profound. They were full of sweet gestures that mattered. I believed it wouldn't be long before he tells me the words that I've been dying to hear. Everything is going to change now.

I am not sure how Adam is going to take this. Would the loving smile on his face turn to hatred when he learns of the pregnancy? He might think that I am tricking him into extending our marriage. Then all the trust and the mutual respect would end.

I tried hard not to cry as I drove to Liv's place. However, as she opened the door for me I couldn't hold my tears anymore.

"What's wrong?" She was shocked to see me like this. "Is Timo okay?"

I nodded and went straight to the living room. Tessa jumped to her feet and came rushing to me, "What happened?" She patted my hand and made me sit, Liv came and joined us on the couch. "What's wrong, Tal?" She asked again, concerned.

I wiped away my tears and took a deep breath, "I am pregnant."

"God, you scared the hell out of me." Liv poked me in the side playfully. "Congratulations."

"But we were careful," I said almost to myself.

"Are you on the pill?" Tessa asked.

"No, but we used condoms."

"Condoms have a two percent birth rate taking into consideration that you never forget to use them," Tessa told me.

"We never..." I wanted to say that we never forgot, but then I realized that it wasn't entirely correct. We did forget, once.

It was on Christmas Eve, I bought sexy lingerie and wore it for Adam, it was my Christmas present for him, and he liked his present very much. Although the news still shook me, I couldn't help smiling at the memory of that night.

"From the look on your face, I can tell you weren't that careful after all," Tessa pointed out.

"But it was only once," I whispered.

They both smiled at me, "It doesn't take more than that to get knocked up. Didn't they teach you this at school?" Liv teased.

"What did Adam say about this? Was he upset?" Tessa asked.

I shook my head and said, "I haven't told him yet."

"When are you going to?"

"I don't know, but soon. I guess."

After a few moments, Liv broke the silence, "I know you weren't expecting this, but maybe this pregnancy is a sign for a new beginning."

"What… what if he doesn't want the baby," I thought out loud.

But they both heard me because they said at the same time, "You did it before. You can do it again."

"But I don't think that Adam is anything like the asshole you were married to," Tessa added and I smiled.

"No, Adam is nothing like Jeff, but even if he didn't want anything to do with the baby, I could do it on my own," I agreed.

Reflexively, I put a hand on my tummy and smiled, "God, I am having a baby."

With the initial shock gone, I realized that I wanted this baby. Maybe it wasn't part of our arrangement, but it was conceived in love from my side at least.

"I am sorry for getting emotional over the whole situation. I didn't mean to ruin our girls' night."

"That is normal. It's called pregnancy hormones," Tessa shrugged and gave me an encouraging smile. "You were in shock, but you'll adjust. You've always adjusted, no matter what's thrown at you."

"Thanks," I gave them both a weak smile.

"Besides, the night isn't over yet. You go and change so that we can get started," Liv said.

True to her word, Liv had set up everything in the living room for our girls' night. The food and the wine, she also brought orange juice and water for me. The three of us sat there eating and enjoying each other's company and they managed to distract me from my thoughts.

"But now we can't get Talia drunk and make her tell us about her sexual adventures," Tessa complained and emptied her wine glass. I could see it wasn't her first; I guessed it wouldn't take much more before she gets tipsy.

"You don't need to get me drunk to tell you that. Which part do you want to know? The mind-blowing jungle sex or the sweet and slow breath-taking sex," I smiled coyly.

"Now she's going to brag. I'll go for part one. I can't remember when last I had that kind of sex," Liv said.

"I assume Peter was the missionary type and he had no imagination in the bedroom," Tessa observed.

"We're not going there," Liv gave her a warning look.

Tessa ignored her and went on, "I don't want to hear about it, and I think there is nothing to hear anyway. I guess he did it fully clothed."

"Tess." I wanted her to stop; I didn't want her to upset Liv.

But Tess didn't get the hint, "You know Peter reminds me so much of Aron. I can't picture any of them naked."

To my surprise, Liv wasn't upset. She asked her somewhat amused, "Why would you want to picture them naked?"

"I don't want to. I hate him you know."

"Who? And how much have you had to drink?" I asked.

"Aron Hamilton, who else? And I am not drunk." She wasn't drunk yet, but she was on her way there. Tessa never talked about her emotions.

"Have you seen him lately?" Liv wanted to know.

"Yeah, I was invited to a party last week, and he was there too. He criticised my dress, my lifestyle and told me that my irresponsible behavior affected his family image. I just told him to go to hell and left the party early," she told us.

Liv and I exchanged worried looks, we also didn't approve of the way Tessa lived after losing Seth. "He's not totally wrong. You can't keep on living the way you do, it's dangerous." I squeezed her hand.

"What's wrong with the way I am living, I don't do relationships. When I need to get laid, I hit a bar and have a one-night-stand. I don't have time or energy for anything else. Besides, I don't do that often," she tried to explain.

"Seth was your act one, sweetie. Someday, you will find love again, but you have to give yourself a chance," I told her.

"Seth was my first and last, I will never, ever, let myself fall again." She shook her head, and a sense of sadness coated the moment.

I pulled her into a hug and squeezed her tightly. Suddenly, the tension in the room was so thick I could cut it with a knife.

Liv and I exchanged a long glance before we changed the conversation to a new topic.

After a while, Liv suggested that we watch a movie and neither Tessa or I objected.

Later that night, I thought about Tessa a lot. I hated the fact that she was still hurting and that I couldn't do anything about it. She and

Seth were so much in love, it wasn't fair that she had to lose him like that. But life goes on, and she must learn to live again.

Thinking about Tessa dragged my thoughts away from my situation. I didn't brood over the baby and what Adam would feel and say about it.

The following morning, I woke up with morning sickness and I realized that confronting Adam was inevitable.

Chapter Twenty
Adam

I had a restless night; I couldn't think of anything other than Talia's pregnancy and the coming baby. The fact that I was about to be a father was overwhelming. I wasn't aware that I wanted to be one until I saw the pregnancy test last night. I needed to know how Talia felt about the baby and what she was going to say about extending our arrangement.

She has to agree.

It was the reasonable thing to do. The new contract would give us eighteen more months; this would be sufficient time for us to decide where we wanted to go from there.

The more I thought about it, the more convinced I became that this was indeed the best option. All I had to do, was get Talia to agree to my proposal.

I went through the new contract one more time while I waited for Talia. I didn't have to wait long, half an hour later I heard her car. She was surprised to find me waiting for her as she came through the door. "You're still here; I thought you were going to the office." She approached, brushing her lips briefly against mine.

I pulled back a little bit so that I could meet her gaze. "I missed my wife, I decided I'd wait for her."

She smiled shyly at me and said, "Your wife missed you too."

"Good, because I missed this," I leaned forward and started to kiss her, REALLY kiss her. Like I've never kissed her before.

I had planned to keep my hands off her until after we had our conversation. But the way she looked and sounded was just too much. As my mouth dominated hers, I found the zipper to her dress and yanked it down.

"Wait! Timo could…"

I didn't give her a chance to finish her sentence, I said between kisses, "Timo is going to spend the day with Josh, Mrs. Smith took the day off to visit her daughter. We have the house to ourselves."

Talia didn't answer. Instead, she tugged my T-shirt up and off. A moment later it was tossed on the floor along with her dress. She was as eager and desperate as I was.

When I lifted her off her feet, she melted against me like hot wax. "I won't make it upstairs," I said as I carried her to the living room and laid her on the nearest couch. "I can't keep my hands off you."

"Then don't," she said breathlessly, "Don't keep your hands off me."

And I didn't. I wanted her warm body, her long, slim lines, and curves. I needed the taste of her filling me as I kissed my way down her body. Talia breathed my name out as my lips brushed her skin in a feather light motion. She reached for me, her hands stroking my back lightly. We were savoring each other. When she cupped my face in her hands, our eyes met, and I felt joy merged with desire.

I kissed her again, slowly this time and she completely melted into the kiss. I felt her fingers thread through my hair as I slid into her. Her gaze held mine as we moved together in a perfect rhythm.

When we both found our release, I realized that I was still pressing her into the couch with my full weight. I lifted myself up, and she rolled herself free. I looked at her as she sat there, beautiful, glowing and smiling at me.

“I missed you last night. Did you and Timo have fun?”

“We sure did, how about you, did you have a good time?”

“Yeah, it was nice, but Tessa had a lot to drink and woke up with a terrible headache this morning,” she said, although she was smiling, I could see that something was bothering her.

“Sorry to hear that, but this isn’t the only thing that’s bothering you,” I frowned.

“Nothing is bothering me. I’m fine, I promise,” she gave me a weak smile.

“Are you sure there is nothing you want to tell me?” I wanted to give her chance to tell me about the pregnancy herself.

Talia was silent for a few moments, and then she finally said, "There is something I need to tell you. Give me a few minutes to change, and we can talk." She picked up my T-shirt and put it on first then she gathered her clothes and left the room.

Twenty minutes later, we were again sitting in the living room - clothes on this time. Talia was quiet; I could see that she was pondering what to say, so I decided to help her. I took her phone and the test from my pocket and gave them to her, "You forgot these last night."

Talia looked down at the test in her hands and back up at me, blushing, "You…you know?"

"Yeah, I found the test last night," I confirmed and smiled at her.

"And you're not mad?" she asked confused.

"Why should I be?"

"Because this wasn't part of our deal." She looked at me, "Our arrangement will end soon."

"Yeah, but we can extend it a little, I'd say for eighteen more months, what do you say?" I asked her and picked up the new contract from the side table.

"What is this?" She hesitated as she took the papers.

"It's a new arrangement. We can go through it now if you like." I tried hard to sound casual, but I was so anxious about her answer.

"Yeah, let's get it out of the way." She was disappointed, I could hear it in her voice.

"I know you're disappointed now, but when you think about it, you'll find that it is the reasonable thing to do," I told her and sat on the couch next to her.

Talia nodded and smiled weakly. She wasn't happy, but she didn't refuse. *That's a good sign,* I thought.

After she went through the first couple of pages, she shook her head, "This is very generous, but if I say yes, it won't be for the money this time."

"But…" I wanted to object, but Talia stopped me.

"No money," she said again.

I couldn't argue anymore, I sat and watched her go through the rest of the contract. She quickly read it and was about to pick up a pen and sign it when something stopped her. "You can't be serious," she shook her head slowly. "You want a DNA test?" She looked horrified.

"This baby is going to be the heir of my empire; I had to be hundred percent sure it's mine." I tried to explain.

"And you're not sure?" She jumped to her feet and tears filled her eyes.

I reached out, but she stepped away from my hands. "Don't you dare touch me." She tore the contract to pieces and threw it on the floor.

Without another word, she left the room. I knew better than to follow her in that condition, so I sat and waited for her to cool off first.

Half an hour later she came down the stairs with her bags.

"What are you doing?"

"I'm leaving. Our time is up anyway; I'll stay at my parents' till I find a house." Her eyes were red, I could see she had been crying.

"Talia, please wait, we can work this out. If you don't want to do the test, it's okay with me."

She shook her head, "It's not the test Adam, but the fact that you asked for it. I would have said yes to your new arrangement. I would have stayed and waited for things to change. But they won't because you don't want to change them."

I didn't respond because she was right; I was comfortable with what we had. I didn't want more.

"What about Timo and the baby?" I heard myself asking.

"You can still take part in their lives if you want. I won't stop you," she said and turned around and walked out of my life.

I didn't follow her. I decided to give her time to calm down. *She'll come back,* I kept telling myself.

*****

A week passed, and Talia didn't come back. She didn't call or take my calls. I went to her office every day, but she wasn't there. I was in a shitty mood all week; my employees tried avoiding me as much as they could. But I didn't care about work. All I cared about was Talia. I let my people keep tabs on her and on what she was doing.

I knew she was looking for houses; I contacted the real estate company she was using, and they sent me a list of all the houses she saw. Among all of them, there was one she liked best, but she couldn't afford it. My first instinct was to buy the house for her, but I decided against it. I knew Talia very well by now, she wouldn't accept it.

I was sitting in my office trying to come up with a plan to make Talia accept the house when I heard the noise outside my office.

I opened the door and saw the last person I was expecting to see, "Sharon, what are you doing here?"

"Adam, darling, I missed you so much." Her eyes lit when she saw me.

"What do you want Sharon?" I asked impatiently.

"I need to talk to you. In private."

I didn't answer, just went back to my office and she rushed in after me. As I closed the door, she came closer and wanted to kiss me. I took a step back and asked her to take a seat. When I was seated behind my desk, I asked her again, "Why are you here Sharon?"

"I want another chance," she said and started to remind me how good and happy we were together.

I sat there looking at her. She was beautiful, but everything about her was fake. Although I let her talk, I wasn't really listening. I was wondering how could I have once loved her.

I found myself comparing my time with her to the life I had with Talia. Only then I realized that I never really loved Sharon. Talia was my first, and she is going to be my last love.

I stood up and smiled at Sharon, who looked hopefully at me. "Thanks a lot for coming to see me today. You made me realize what I really miss."

She smiled triumphantly and straightened her back to highlight her fake breasts, then whispered, "And what do you miss?"

"My wife, I miss my wife, and I am going to get her back," I grinned.

"Adam, you can't be serious, this girl is nothing compared to me."

"You're right, Talia is nothing like you. Have a good life, Sharon," I went to the door and opened it for her. She stomped out of my office. Her face was purple with rage. Sharon wasn't used to being rejected.

After she left, I had one thing on my mind.

How am I going to win Talia back?

Chapter Twenty-One
Talia

It had been a week, seven long days since I left Adam. He called several times every day, but I didn't answer. I was still staying at my parents. I didn't go to the office either; I wasn't ready to face him yet. I knew I wouldn't be able to avoid him for long; he was my baby's father. Unlike Timo's father, Adam was going to be there for the baby. We wouldn't be married any longer, but this baby was going to connect us for a lifetime, and I had to come to terms with that.

One of the advantages of staying with my parents was that my mom took care of Timo, while I licked my wounds. The first three days were the worst; I did nothing but cry, sleep, and brood. I thought about Adam a lot, our time together and our arrangement. I asked myself over and over if the money was worth the pain. The answer was the same every time, a big NO.

After I cried my eyes out, I concluded that my time with Adam was worth the pain. I wouldn't take any moment back. He gave me a lot more than money; he brought the old Talia back to life.

When I married Jeff, I was young, joyful and full of life. However, shortly after our marriage, all this had changed. I wasn't the same person after the divorce. During our short marriage, Jeff had managed to squash my confidence and my self-esteem.

He made me feel so small that I questioned myself and my abilities but he didn't break my heart; I realized that now. What I suffered after my divorce wasn't a broken heart, it was a wounded spirit. Although my parents, Timo's birth and my work helped me, I wasn't completely healed.

Adam did that. He managed to heal me. With him I felt wanted, cherished and loved. Although he didn't love me the way I wanted, I knew Adam loved me in his own way. I realized that I couldn't blame him for my broken heart; falling in love wasn't part of our deal. It wasn't his fault that I loved him so much.

I felt better when I reached this conclusion; I wasn't upset with Adam anymore but the deep pain inside me didn't lessen.

However, after the first three days, I realized that I had to live with the pain. I had to be strong for Timo and the coming baby.

I called a real-estate company and started looking for houses. Of the six properties I saw in the past four days, there was only one I liked. I was disappointed when I learned the price. It was far more than I could afford.

I couldn't believe it when Kate, the real-estate agent called earlier and said that the owner was willing to give me a better deal. I said yes right away when she suggested a meeting the next morning.

Excited, I went to find Timo to share the news with him. I found him in my old room. He was busy drawing something, but he quickly hid it when he saw me coming. "Hi honey, aren't you going to show me what you're drawing?" I leant in to kiss him.

He shook his head and said, "It's a surprise."

"Fine, my surprise will have to wait too," I teased.

"Are we going back to live with dad?" he asked promptly; his eyes full of hope. Timo loved Adam; he called him dad, which was new for me. I didn't realize how much our separation would have an impact on him. It broke my heart that I had to disappoint him.

"No baby, but I am going to sign the contract to buy our new house tomorrow. You're going to love it there," I said and patted his shoulder.

"Is dad going to live with us there?" he asked again.

"No, but he'll come see you, and you can go visit him."

"But it's not the same; I miss him, mom."

I reached for him, took him in my arms, and planted a kiss on his head. "Adam can't live with us, but that doesn't mean that he won't love you anymore. You know that, don't you?"

"Yeah, I know," he said shortly, and I could see he was upset.

"Everything is going to be fine baby, I promise," I said and rushed out of the room.

That night I cried myself to sleep, I didn't know that Timo was going to get hurt. I never thought he would get so attached to Adam. *Now my son is hurt, and it's all my fault.*

In the morning I felt a bit better, I was hoping that the new house would cheer Timo up. I quickly got dressed and went to meet Kate in the house.

When I arrived there, Kate's car wasn't there. Instead, I found a brand-new SUV in the driveway. It was full of baby stuff. *Oh my God, the house, someone has beaten me to it.* I rushed inside to see what was going on.

The front door was open, I stepped inside, and I found Adam standing there smiling at me. "Adam, what are you doing here? Where is Kate? Whose car is parked outside?"

"Kate had to go; she asked me to give you this. As for the car, it's a present." He gave me the car keys and the contract to the house. It was paid in full, and it belonged to me.

I shook my head and said, "You can't just buy me a house and a car and think it will fix everything. I won't take them; you know that."

"I know the house won't fix everything, but I was hoping this would," He took out prenup contract that I'd signed from his briefcase and tore it in two.

I looked at him confused, and I didn't know what to say. When I said nothing, he took out another paper and gave it to me, "I have a few cards up my sleeve."

I looked at the paper; it was a picture of the four of us; Adam, me, Timo and the baby. I recognized Timo's handwriting; *Please say YES, mom*. I looked at the picture and back at Adam and murmured, "But how? When? He must have drawn this yesterday."

Adam took another step to close the distance between us. "He finished it yesterday and threw it out the window. I was there to catch it."

"You were at my parents' house last night! And Timo knew?"

"It was our little secret," he grinned.

"What are you trying to say, Adam, because I am not sure I follow," I was confused.

"You were right when you said that I didn't want to change anything in our arrangement." He looked at me and continued, "I thought it was the only way to keep my heart safe, but when you left last week, I realized it was too late for that, I am already so deep in. You've got me by the gut, by the balls, by the heart."

"You said the heart," I whispered, and he nodded.
"I love you although I tried so hard not to fall for you. But you made it impossible just by being you. I guess I knew it the first time we slept together; that was why I panicked and tried to keep my distance. I wanted it to be just sex."

As he spoke my eyes filled with happy tears.

"But it was never just sex; it was a hell of a lot more than that. You worked your way into my heart, and I enjoyed every moment of it."

"The baby is..." Adam didn't let me finish. He placed a finger over my lips.

"Shhh...I know it's mine, but this is not about the baby. You are my real prize; the baby is a nice bonus." Adam smiled and placed a tender kiss on my lips.

"I want to marry you. I want to be a father to Timo and the baby. This house is a symbol of a new beginning." He took a little box out of his pocket and gave it to me. My breath caught as I saw the ring. "I chose this one myself. It is not as big as the first one, but it's simple, beautiful and pure just like you." He placed the ring on my finger and lifted my hands to his lips and kissed it tenderly.

"Say yes, say you'll marry me."

"God, Adam we're already married."

He smiled and cupped my face in his hands. "Is that a yes?"

God, I loved him so much. It was me who closed the distance between us this time. I placed my lips on his and kissed him softly. "I Love you too."

"Say yes."

"I thought I already did."

Adam pulled me into his arms and deepened our promising kiss. When I pulled back to catch my breath he said with a grin, "You know this house has only one master bedroom. Now you have to live with my snoring."

"I thought you didn't snore."

"I lied, I snore, kick and wake up with this every morning." He took my hand and placed it on the bulge between his legs so that I could feel the extent of his desire.

"I think I like the last part the most," I gave him a cocky smile.

"Good because there is no going back now."

"No, there is no going back," I said and melted into Adam's arms. My only thought was that Adam was mine forever.

The End

Coming soon

The Agreement
BOOK TWO IN THE SEATTLE BILLIONAIRES SERIES
NORA FORD

The Agreement

Book two in the Seattle Billionaires series

Nora Ford

Chapter One
Tessa

I got up with a heavy heart this morning. Today is not like any other day. It's the third anniversary of Seth's death. Three years have passed since the day I lost everything. That day I didn't only lose the man I loved and was ready to spend the rest of my life with, but I also lost my baby that I never had the chance to see. And it was all my fault.

I was the one driving the damn car. It should have been me who died on that day but I survived the accident. I woke up from two weeks of an induced coma to find out that I had lost them both, Seth and the baby. He left me, and I didn't even have a chance to say goodbye.

I still don't know what was worse, not being there when he died or spending the last few days of his short life waiting for a miracle to happen. Seth suffered internal injuries that caused irreversible kidney failure; he waited for a donor. But life isn't fair; there was no available kidney from a donor match, he died a week later.

The doctors had said that the accident didn't leave any serious damages and I could still have babies, however, I knew that wasn't possible anymore. A baby had to be conceived in love. I wasn't able to love. The pain and the loss I felt when Seth died were unbearable. I was consumed by grief. I felt guilty all the time, guilty about living.

After a few months, I stopped crying and started to deal with my loss. I now work, eat and sleep. I even have sex when the mood strikes and my time allows it. But it's nothing more than a physical act. I am unable to love - at least not again.

I know I wouldn't survive another loss. Since Seth's death, I've worked hard to put the pieces of my shredded heart back together. I have a few rules to stay in control of my life and most importantly my heart.

I don't date or do relationships and never spend the night with any of my one-night-stands. Once the sex had finished, I'd leave their bed. That way I get my physical need without getting emotionally attached. This is my life and I like it this way.

I got used to my new life. Although I never stopped grieving, I learned to live with the pain. Today, however, my loneliness is more intense. Thoughts of Seth and the life we had together, the children we'll never have keep going through my mind all day.

I usually spend this day working myself into the ground, but it's different this time. This year I am going to the Hamiltons. I've been nervous the whole week, since my phone call with Grace. She called last week and told me about the meeting this evening.

Grace is Seth's mother. Although it has been three years since the accident, I still have a close relationship with Seth's family, especially Grace. She had three sons, Jason, Aron, and Seth. For her, I have always been the daughter she didn't have. I also love her so much and consider her a second mother.

However, the warm relationship I have with her can't change the way Aron and I feel about each other. Aron is Seth's older brother, and he hates me. I don't know why, but it was clear from the moment we first met. I used to ignore his hostile attitude towards me when Seth was alive. Now I try to avoid him as much as I can. It's not going to be possible this evening though.

He is going to be present at the meeting. It's about the reading of Seth's will. Seth wanted it that way; for his shares in the Hamilton Group to be finally distributed three years after his death.

I don't care about the money; I have enough. I own a beautiful apartment, a new car and have a good job. Since completing my residency, I practice as a general obstetrician and gynecologist at the University of Washington Medical Center. I still work crazy hours, but I need to be busy all the time.

I loved Seth and not his money, no matter how much I would inherit, it won't bring him back. I wished I could skip this gathering, but I had to attend; Seth wanted me to be there.

After brooding all day over the meeting, I finally showered and changed and forced myself to drive to the Hamiltons.

Grace opened the door for me and welcomed me with a warm smile and a hug. "Come in my dear. Brian, Jason and Aron are waiting in my study."

"Am I late? Mr. Collins is already here?" Brian Collins is the Hamilton's lawyer and will read the will.

"It's fine, dear, he has just arrived," Grace said and led me to her office. When I entered the room, all three men rose up to greet me. "Ms. Jones," Brian extended his hand, I briefly shook it. "Mr. Collins. Nice to see you again."

I turned to Jason who pulled me into a brotherly hug. "Tessa, long time no see."

I gave him a warm smile, "You know where to find me. You're the one who's too busy chasing skirts."

"Honey, I chase no one, they are the ones who chase me," he grinned.

Before I could respond, Aron, who was standing next to Jason gave us an irritated look and said, "If you too have finished, we need to get started. Brian doesn't have all night."

I ignored him and sat on the couch next to Jason. "What's his problem now? How can someone be that rude? He didn't even greet me," I murmured to myself. Jason must have heard me, he squeezed my hand and whispered, "He got up on the wrong side of the bed."

I nodded as I looked at Aron who was as grumpy as always.

At that moment Grace came and sat opposite us. She smiled at me and gave Aron a warning look, "Brian, can we start now."

"Sure, but before I start, I need to ask Aron and Ms. Jones a question," Brian said.

"Fine, go ahead," I heard Aron saying.

"Are you in any serious relationships at the moment?" Brian asked Aron.

"Not that it is any of your business but, no," Aron said impatiently.

Brian nodded and turned to me, "Ms. Jones, are you in a serious relationship?"

"Are you asking me out?" I gave him a cocky smile.

"Believe me if I were twenty years younger and not happily married, I would be honored to do that," he gave me a warm smile. Brian looked much younger than his sixty years of age, and within the constraints of a business suit, he still looked lean and able. If he weren't married, I would have flirted a little more with him.

I was about to tell him that, but Aron didn't give me a chance to say anything. He took a deep breath and said impatiently, "I can't see how these questions are relevant to the will reading."

"You will understand in a moment how relevant they are," Brian said shortly and looked again at me. "So, are you in a serious relationship at the moment, Ms. Jones?"

I felt all eyes were on me, waiting for my answer. I quickly shook my head, "No, I am not in any relationship."

"It seems that Seth knew both of you very well. He wanted you to equally share seventy percent of his shares in the Hamilton Group. Mrs. Hamilton and Jason would have fifteen percent each. But there is one condition," Brian told us.

"What condition?" Aron asked.

"Aron and Ms. Jones have to get married immediately and stay married for at least a year," Brian said and waited for our response. Aron was the first to break the silence, "And if we don't?"

"In that case, all Seth's shares will go to your cousin Jacob Hamilton."

"You can't be serious, Seth knew how Jacob felt about us, the man has been trying to destroy us for years," Aron growled.

"I am sorry, but this was Seth's last will. You both have a week to decide. If you don't agree, I have to contact Jacob." He said and gave Aron and me two letters. I took mine and watched Aron taking his. We both said nothing.

"I honestly don't understand why Seth did that but read the letters. He might have explained everything in them," Brian told us.

"Thanks, Brian, you will hear from me soon. Please don't contact Jacob before I call you," I heard Aron saying.

"Sure, I hope you two make the right decision," Brian said to Aron and me on his way out.

I didn't say anything. I was still in shock. I put the letter in my purse and left the room. Aron and Jason were engaged in a conversation, they didn't notice me leaving, and it was better this way. I didn't want to talk to anyone.

However, Grace saw me leaving. She came after me, "I'll walk you to your car, dear." I didn't object but I didn't say anything either. I didn't know what to say or how to react. I had to think, and I needed to do it alone. Grace sensed how I was feeling; she didn't push me to speak. We walked together in silence. When we reached my car, she pulled me into a tight hug and whispered, "No matter what you decide, you will always be a daughter to me."

"Thank you, Grace." I gave her a weak smile before I got into my car and drove off.

Chapter Two
Aron

The moment Tessa entered the room, my body reacted to her the same way it did when I first saw her at a party eight years ago. I was twenty-five back then and doing my MBA at Harvard Business School.

My stomach growled loudly as I caught sight of her, a stunning dark-haired beauty. Mesmerized by her bewitching blue eyes, I stood and watched her laughing with another guy; her brilliant blue eyes were alive with joy. She took my breath away.

I saw her small hands adjusting the tiny straps of her sexy as sin dress at the shoulder. My cock stirred, as I imagined that delicate hand wrapped around it. Although she wasn't my type, I couldn't stop myself from staring at her. She was small and lean with a perfect figure, her rounded breasts weren't big but large on her petite frame. I hadn't felt such an attraction to a woman before. When I asked a friend about her, I learned that she was a first-year medical student. I didn't try to talk to her; the age difference discouraged me.

I wasn't the only one who noticed her. Seth saw her too. Unlike me, he wasn't hesitant to approach her. He left the party with her phone number. A week later they were dating.

Seth was studying medicine at Harvard as well, but he was three years her senior. After a few months of dating, they moved in together. When Tessa finished her studies, they both moved back to Seattle. They were supposed to get married but the wedding never took place. Seth died two months before their big day.

All those years, Tessa never knew how I felt about her. Even after Seth's death, I never made a move on her. It didn't feel right; to me, she was Seth's woman.

I was jealous though, when I saw her flirting with Jason. I gave them a disapproving look and heard myself saying, ""If you too have finished, we need to get started. Brian doesn't have all night."

Tessa ignored me and sat on the couch next to Jason. She thought I was rude, but I couldn't treat her any other way without showing how I felt, so I made it a habit to be on my worst behavior when she was around.

I wanted this meeting to end; I got impatient when Brain started to ask about our love lives. "I can't see how these questions are relevant to the will reading," I told him.

"You will understand in a moment how relevant they are," Brian said shortly and looked at Tessa again, "So, are you in a serious relationship at the moment, Ms. Jones?" he asked her one more time. I don't know why but I was relieved when I heard Tessa saying, "No, I am not in any relationship."

When Brian dropped the bomb and told us about the condition in Seth's will, we all stayed silent. Suddenly, the tension in the room was so thick one could cut it with a knife. I was the first to recover from the shock. I asked Brian, "And if we don't?"

"In that case, all Seth's shares will go to your cousin Jacob Hamilton."

"You can't be serious, Seth knew how Jacob felt about us, the man has been trying to destroy us for years," I yelled.

I was furious. I couldn't understand what Seth was thinking when he wrote this. Jacob was the enemy. When our grandfather died, Jacob's father didn't want anything to do with the family business, so he sold his shares in the Hamilton Group to my dad. The Hamilton name and fortune weren't as massive then as they are today. Back then we owned only twenty hotels. Unlike my dad, who worked hard and managed to multiply our fortune several times, his brother lost all his money gambling.

Jacob didn't take it well; he tried to take us to court, but he failed. After that, he made several attempts to take loans using our assets but when we stopped him, he threatened us. That was a week before Seth's accident. We believed he had something to do with it, but the police couldn't prove it.

Brian interrupted my thoughts, "I am sorry, but this was Seth's last will. You both have a week to decide. If you don't agree, I have to contact Jacob," he said and gave Tessa and me two letters, we took them and said nothing.

"I honestly don't understand why Seth did that, but read the letters, he might have explained everything in them," Brian suggested.

"Thanks, Brian, you will hear from me soon. Please don't contact Jacob before I call you," I requested.

"Sure, I hope you two will make the right decision," Brian said to Tessa and me on his way out.

The moment Brian left the room, Jason turned to me and asked, "What are you going to do? You wouldn't allow Jacob to take our money, would you?"

"Of course not. I am not paying a cent to that bastard. This is our money. Dad and I worked so hard for it," I said and meant every word.

I took over the family business seven years ago, after dad's sudden death. Back then the Hamilton Group had over two hundred hotels. Now our portfolio includes more than two thousand properties with hotels and resorts in a hundred countries. Last year the Hamilton Group was on Forbes America's Largest Private Companies List. I will be damned if I let Jacob take thirty percent of all this.

I looked at Tessa who was staring at the letter in her hand; she was still in shock. Jason was talking to me but I wasn't listening, I was watching her leave. Although I wanted to stop her, I knew it wasn't wise to speak to her now.

When Tessa left, I turned back to Jason, "Sorry, what were you saying?"

"How could Seth do that? I don't understand," Jason asked confused.

"I honestly don't get it either," I said and looked at the letter in my hand.

"Aren't you going to open it?" My mom asked the minute she returned from walking Tessa to her car.

I looked at the letter again and said nothing, I just nodded and opened it. I took a deep breath then I started reading:

Hey Bro,

I know you're pissed off at me right now. But I don't have much time, and I couldn't come up with a better plan to bring Tessa and you together. You will do anything to prevent Jacob from taking our money.

Don't be surprised. I know you have had feelings for Tessa since you first saw her. Knowing you so well, I am sure you haven't acted on those feelings yet. I guess you never will out of your misplaced sense of loyalty.

I don't blame you. Tessa is the most amazing woman I've ever met. She is beautiful inside and out. I don't want her to spend the rest of her life alone. I want her to love and be loved again. You love her, I am certain of it. I am giving you a chance to show her how much. Make her happy. You have my blessing. Seth

"That's insane," I said almost to myself after I finished reading. Both mom and Jason gave me a questioning look, but I ignored it and gave them the letter.

When they finished, mom was the first to speak. "So, you'll do it. Won't you?" She raised her brows in question.

"You wouldn't let Jacob take thirty percent of everything we own, would you?" Jason added.

I ignored Jason's question and looked at my mom, "You don't seem to be surprised. Did Seth tell you about his plan?"

"No, he didn't tell me. But I knew he was planning something that involved Tessa. I didn't know what," Mom assured me.

"And what makes you sure that Tessa will agree? She was in shock when she left. I am sure that she didn't like the idea. The woman hates me for God's sake."

"That's ridiculous. Of course, Tessa doesn't hate you. She tries to avoid you because you're always giving her a hard time." Mom carried on, "She will agree, Tessa hates Jacob. She believes like the rest of us that he was the one behind the accident."

I couldn't argue with that. Tessa hated no one as much as she hated Jacob. She didn't only lose Seth in the accident, but she lost her unborn child. She might never speak of her baby, but I was sure she was still hurting. However, it wasn't right to use the way she felt about Jacob to make her agree. "Even if she agrees, this whole thing is wrong. You can't just trick two people into marriage."

"Why? Don't you have feelings for her? Seth gave you the opportunity to win her heart," she asked.

"That is not the point. What Seth did isn't right. He chose for her. Don't you think that Tessa has the right to choose?" I was furious. As much as I craved Tessa and wanted to marry her, I didn't like the whole thing.

"She's had three years to choose. But she hasn't. Instead, she's just built armor to protect herself."

"Are you saying that after three years she loses her rights?" I asked in a perplexed tone.

"No, of course not. But do you like the way she has been living the past three years? This is not the life Seth wanted for her, and it's definitely not what I wish for her."

Of course, I didn't like her lifestyle, but that wasn't the point. "Mom, Tessa is a grown woman; she is twenty-seven. She can live her life the way she wants."

Mom shook her head, "She is young, beautiful and now she is going to be very wealthy. She could easily fall prey to the wrong man. Do you want that to happen?"

I didn't answer. Indeed, I didn't want that; I couldn't even imagine her showing interest in another man.

When I didn't respond, Jason said, "You overthink, you need to act. Seth knew you needed a push and he gave it to you."

Before I could respond, mom added, "You're a good businessman. You know that it pays to grab what's good and right when you can. Tessa is the real prize, not the money. I'm sure you could crack her armor and wiggle your way into her heart." Mom patted my hand and stood to leave. She stopped when she reached the door and looked at me for a long moment. Finally, she smiled and said, "Aron, I'd put my money on you."

"I guess that's our cue to leave," Jason said and rose up.

We walked in silence to our cars. When we reached them, Jason patted me on the shoulder. "So, I guess congratulations are in order," he grinned.

"She hasn't said yes yet," I reminded him.

"Don't worry, man. She will," he said and got into his car.

After Jason drove away, I sat in my car for a while. I needed some time to clear my mind and think. I pondered the opportunity that Seth gave me. Wasn't that what I always wanted? A chance.

I knew that breaking down Tessa's defences wouldn't be easy, but it was one challenge I was happy to accept.

I slipped my car into drive and navigated out of the drive way. The whole way home I couldn't push the images from my mind. Tessa, naked in my bed was the only thing that popped into my traitorous mind.

Acknowledgments

Thank you so much for reading my book. If you enjoyed Adam and Talia's story, please wait for Aron and Tessa's story in *The Agreement*

Thank you to the following people for their help and contributions in the making of

The Seattle Billionaires series 1

The Arrangement:

Beta Readers: Dalia & Hoda

Copyediting: Laila

Cover design: Matt stone

Made in United States
Orlando, FL
21 January 2023